A GIANT'S HOSTAGE

"Let Sena speak," Sam said into the telephone.

"Certainly," the voice replied calmly. "As I re-marked before, she's busy. I'll see if she wants to talk to you. Hang on."

Silence. . . . The silence stretched out, and for the first time of which he was aware, Sam began to worry. There was something unsettling about the calmness with which that man clung to his story and his course, as though it were indeed possible that he and he alone was the only loyal giant and the rest of them traitors and fools. And since even he would hardly go so far as to let Sena speak, he must be using these moments in some other way—

"Here she is."

"Sam?" Sena's voice said quietly.

"Yes . . . yes, Sena."

"I'm all right. There's no reason for you to worry about me at all. He's got a gun on me—"

JAMES BLISH

TITANS' DAUGHTER

With a New Introduction by Virginia Kidd

AVON
PUBLISHERS OF BARD, CAMELOT, DISCUS AND FLARE BOOKS

AVON BOOKS
A division of
The Hearst Corporation
959 Eighth Avenue
New York, New York 10019

First Avon Printing, November, 1981

To Mother and Tom

Acknowledgments: About half of this novel first appeared as BEANSTALK by James Blish in an anthology called *Future Tense,* copyright 1952 by Kendall Foster Crossen; as GIANTS IN THE EARTH by James Blish in the January 1956 issue of *Science Fiction Stories,* copyright 1956 by Columbia Publications, Inc.: and as BEANSTALK in the British edition of *Galactic Cluster,* copyright 1960 by James Blish. This novel version, like the original, could not have come into being without the extensive contributions of my wife, Virgina Kidd.

James Blish

"And the LORD said, My spirit shall not always strive with man, for that he also *is* flesh: yet his days shall be an hundred and twenty years.

"There were giants in the earth in those days; and also after that, when the sons of God came in unto the daughters of men, and they *bare* children to them, and the same *became* mighty men which *were* of old, men of renown."

—The First Book of Moses,
called GENESIS

INTRODUCTION

James Blish was a polymath, a perfectionist, and a poet, as well as a fierce and fearsome critic, and a novelist and short story writer of real distinction.

One of his dicta—not, I think, original with him—was that writing is done out of clinical necessity. He hardly ever talked about Art with a capital A (although he accomplished it now and again). He invoked very few muses (only once that I recall—and then in a poem). What he was talking about was that compulsion that drove him back to the typewriter (after a full day of writing at his place of business) every night of the week, every day of the weekend, and caused him to cut vacations short (or to spend them churning out an entire novel: *Warriors of Day*, for instance). He had a very high opinion of my writing ability, and yet he has a body of work to his credit while I have virtually none. He found creative writing absolutely necessary; I find it exceedingly difficult. He tried all kinds of tricks to get me to write more. It was easy for me to throw a paragraph into something of his if he asked me to, and he occasionally did—witness Polly Follmer. It was a pleasure, once, to provide a lacking chapter when he was up against a deadline—witness much of Dee Hazleton and all of the game-playing episode in *The Triumph of Time*. (There was even one ironic incident which occurred when he had promised, as a moderately loyal alumnus, to do a short-short story for his fraternity's magazine and found himself with not one minute to spare when due date was upon him. The only short-short story idea in the house was a minor piece called "Masks," and I had just written it. I offered it to him because the story was not important, but the deadline was. That was the one set of circumstances, however, where his byline and only his byline could be used. He had sufficient of an attack of conscience so that he ran it through the typewriter one more time—

noticeably strengthening the ending—before turning it in. That's the closest I ever came to "belonging" to a men's Greek letter society; had they known, I suppose his brothers would have disowned him as well as me.) However, he wrote voluminously and I very little. I hardly ever felt that clinical necessity, and yet I know exactly what he was talking about because I lived intimately with its manifestations for nineteen years, most of which were very happy. I am exceedingly proud of the fact that, after our divorce, he dedicated his best book, *Doctor Mirabilis*, to me.

In case you missed the small print in the *Acknowledgments*, James Blish said, "This novel, like the original, could not have come into being without the extensive contributions of my wife, Virginia Kidd." "Extensive" is a relative term; while I gave close reading to every word of *Doctor Mirabilis*, I did not write one syllable. Generally speaking, though, I was Jim's first reader, and I was very good at it. I might argue the occasional word, the turn of a phrase, as often as half a dozen times per session. (I saw short stories when they were complete, books chapter by chapter.) Once in half a dozen books, I might question the logic or inevitability of a scene. He always listened and he usually adopted my suggestions. To a perfectionist like James Blish, that's a lot of changes to introduce in manuscripts considered complete. But "extensive" does seem to me to be overstating the case. I do not count spelling corrections as changes. Like many good writers, he was shaky in some areas of orthography—he could spell the hard words; it was easy words on which he came a cropper. My contributions were usually those of a very silent partner.

If he had thought of *Titans' Daughter* as a book about a woman, he would have been kidding himself. He was aware of how difficult he found it to attempt a female point of view. It was not until 1966, in "How Beautiful With Banners," that he forced himself to take that hurdle. At the end of 1951, when he wrote "Beanstalk," and during 1960, when he expanded that novella into the book, he was still at the stage of writing all around the problem—like Ford Madox Ford spiraling in on an event from multiple viewpoints, Blish made Sena the central exemplar of polyploidism rather than the central character. Thus the book becomes a sterling example of the roving viewpoint. He used

his author's omniscience like the eye of a camera. Instead
of limiting himself to those events that could be seen by
the woman who might in other hands have been the pro-
tagonist, he went to where the action was, describing what
went down from the vantage point of Dr. Fred's head,
Sam's, Maurey's, and only occasionally and briefly Sena's.

As a writer, James Blish was a disciplined packrat and
a gleeful magpie. He was also a superlative craftsman.
Outside of the genre—among his peers in public relations
and journalism—he was acknowledged to be one of the
three best and most rigorous science writers on the East
Coast (and, I privately thought, in the whole world). At
home, in his science fiction, there was plenty of room not
only for the odd fact but also the outrageous fancy. In
any event, nothing happened at the office or at home that
did not turn up in his writing. Everything was grist to
Jim's mill. How many people know (or care) that the
pragmatist, Charles S. Peirce (pronounced Purse), whose
name whizzes by once in *Titans' Daughter*, lived and
worked one mile up the road from us, here in Milford?
(Peirce himself was dead before we moved to Pennsylvania,
but Jim passed the historical marker in front of his house
just about every day, and I would have made book that
Peirce would turn up sooner or later in a book that Jim
made. I would have won.) For another instance, there
were "Take me to your leader" jokes innumerable in the
late Forties. One of them concerned the astronaut who
discovered a forty-foot-tall woman. "Take me to your lad-
der," he said. "I'll see your leader later." I do believe that
joke engendered Sena—a lovely transformation.

Back in the early days we wrote sports stories: baseball,
hockey, football . . . for, if you relish the historical note,
one-half cent a word. (Jim wrote a lot of them; I only
wrote a few, plus a couple of Westerns and love stories;
Jim would touch neither.) The formulation, in Kelland's
strategy, "Four or five cross-bucks, two rudimentary spinners, and a few laterals—all, in essence, straight power
plays," does not come out of any experience on the football field. It does come out of years of researching and
writing pulp magazine sports fiction. Jim Blish handled
that jargon as, had he been a different kind of American
boy, he might have handled a football; he grasped it surely,
ran with it, and scored.

Even earlier while still in college, he had been trained as a limno-biologist. He switched to the humanities when he realized that he was physically unfit for a career as a research scientist. He suffered all his adult life from what he referred to as an intention tremor, already marked when I met him, fresh out of the army and enrolled in Columbia's graduate school. His hands shook slightly but unremittingly.

He had an excellent set of dissection tools left from his biological studies at Rutgers, and a great deal of knowledge of biology, shorelines and interfaces, and genetics. To that basic training, he appended constant study in the fields of physics, medicine, abstruse mathematics, and any subject that was making scientific news. There was also a deep and abiding interest in music as listener and musicologist. In sum, he could solder a joint on the stereo set (at great risk because of those trembling fingers), he played pretty good French horn, and he had a large refracting telescope which he lugged out into the back yard on winter nights.

Otherwise, all the action was in his head and at his typewriter, because he could not manage the simplest scientific experiment with his treacherous hands. On the other hand, he could play "Universe" with the best of them!

His grist-to-my-mill cast of mind accounts for the visible influence of Joyce in *A Case of Conscience* and for our first dog, Trouble, turning up as Decibelle in *Titans' Daughter*. (As a matter of fact, the pun in the puppy's name is also straight out of James Joyce.) Though Jim was much younger than Dr. Fred, he was painting an idealised self-portrait there. The old man stabbing at the swinging needle to test his reflexes is Jim as he would have liked to have been. The reason I can hear Dr. Fred saying, "Now *there's* a phrase I loathe. Nothing is ever 'as simple as that,' " is because I heard Jim inveigh against the phrase, pungently. Often.

The polymath was a prophet without honor in his own country, in that his father berated him for being such a dilettante. Myself, I preferred to think of him as a Renaissance man, talented in many and disparate fields.

Once, I think as a joke, Jim said it was his ambition to have everything he wrote be a sequel to everything else he had written or would write. He never quite got around to that feat of connectivity, but certainly here are interweavings, cross references, and in-jokes galore. At the same time that he always searched for the exact word, he loved and understood the uses of ambiguity. (As just one double-example, I offer Maurey's speech at the end of Chapter VI: "Check," and Sam's identical message to Sena, later.) More importantly, at his lamentably early death, he left a body of work worthy of respect in and out of the field—and a couple of novels that will surely outlast this century.

—*Virginia Kidd*
Milford, Pennsylvania, 1981

BOOK ONE

I

The girl who came out of the university's Biology Hall was heroically built. From a distance, her body might have been called slim, even slight. But beside the two ugly pseudo-Greek statues which flanked the building, her height showed.

She was at least eight feet tall.

She looked indecisively down the long rank of wide steps, her eyes slitted like a sleepy cat's against the morning sunlight. At the foot of the steps, a small knot of students stopped gossiping, and heads turned toward her. Sena knew the hostility in that silence.

She went down the steps, mincing over them like a dandy. They had not been laid for such a slender goddess; the risers should have been two inches higher for her, the platforms nearly that much broader. As she approached them, the students pointedly turned their backs and examined the state of the weather.

"Damned lummoxes—" somebody muttered.

"Everybody over nine feet tall please leave the room," said someone who had read his Carroll.

Sena had heard it all before, but it still hurt. It was hard not to say "Out of the way, pygmies," or in some other way make a virtue of difference.

Some of the giants had done that, in their hot-headed youth: a group that had gotten notions of superiority not only to ordinary diploid human beings, but to Dr. Fred himself. Their end had not been pretty, but it had been edifying. Dr. Fred told that story often.

"Don't get the idea," he said, "that you're above your diploid fellows just because you can look down on them physically. The day may come when chromosome-doubling will be commonplace. If that day comes, it will come because the process has real advantages over normal reproduction; but those advantages are yet to be proven. If you want to see them proven, don't give yourselves airs—or you won't survive to see."

These days the giants listened to Dr. Fred. He had made the giants. He was very old now, and could be expected to die before the year was out, for his high blood pressure had lately turned malignant; but somehow the giants did not expect him to die. He was a man apart from the other diploids; it seemed impossible that their physical limitations could apply to him—

Careful, careful! The shortness of the diploid lifespan was not necessarily a drawback. That kind of thinking led to paranoia.

Sena passed the students, allowing herself the useless defense of pretending that she hadn't seen them. Like most of the giants, Sena felt vaguely uneasy among them, like a parent in Toytown.

Yet it was more than that. The tallest buildings in the world were not tall enough for her, for even the tallest of buildings had doorways—doorways which would not admit a giantess unless she stooped. The whole of human civilization seemed waiting to be rebuilt, bigger and better, cleaner and higher.

And the time! The giants had so much of it. Their lifespans had not yet been measured, for, thus far, none of them had died except by violence. (That qualification always, so far, meant the Pasadena pogrom—the entire insurgent group on the West Coast, whose pride did not go before their fall or after. The enormous installation they had built cooperatively and without diploid aid as their home turned out to be their funeral pyre and their monument. Laid out in the shape of a gigantic Greek cross, it flamed throughout their crucifixion and smoked for days afterward. That long-shafted T had brought them nothing but hatred and destruction. Dr. Fred kept photographs around to prove it.

(He had had occasion sometimes in the fifteen years since Pasadena to remind his more biddable children that mere existence was ostentation enough, beyond which they must be circumspect.)

Dr. Fred estimated that—unmolested—they should live to be a minimum of 150 years old, more than twice as long as the average diploid human. The one-in-a-thousand tetraploid adult organisms produced by nature, mostly in

Lamarck's evening primrose, lived six times their normal
span; and the first synthetic tetraploids had proven to be
almost as long-lived.

Of course, the very first synthetic tetraploids had been
plants—*Datura*, the common chickweed, developed at
Smith College in 1937. The U.S. Department of Agricul-
ture had later extended the process profitably to food plants
of many kinds. It was the work on rabbits and pigs conducted by Haggquist and his associates at Stockholm's
Karolinska Institute, however, which had proven artificial
polyploidy possible in animals; from that momentous day
in 1950, the road leading to Sena was clear.

For Sena, who was not yet thirty, the whole small world
was in the throes of an endless spring-tide: a youth that
would last more than a century, with toy bridges and
houses and roadplanes clustered at her feet, and more than
time enough to learn everything one needed to know, and
the high-browed, god-like figures of lovers striding through
the narrow streets of diploid man. . . .

The world waited, flooded with delicate greenness that
would never die.

"Sena!"

She turned. Sam Ettinger, the young, black-haired radiation expert, was running after her, traversing the cement
squares in long bounds. The students scattered up the
steps to watch him pass.

"Hello, Sam."

He pulled up, smiling. His eyes crinkled at the corners.
He had a way of looking at people as one might look at a
sleeping tiger cub—with curiosity and admiration, yet with
a certain wariness.

"You're very aloof these days," he said. "One would
think we weren't committed to each other for this cycle."

She reached out for his hands.

"Sam, don't. There is always so much to think about;
you know that. How was the house?"

His mouth drew down at the corners, and he looked
uneasily away. It was not, probably that he wanted—or
needed—privacy any less than she did, but that notions of
privacy differ. He was wholly at ease with the tetras' vacation arrangements, himself, but he did not believe that
Sena ever would be. Well, there it was. He had grown up
a Williamsite, she had come to it late and self-conscious.

Because of her scruples and because he wanted to please
her, he must have gone to look at twenty houses (and
she at twenty more) but the outcome was always the same.

"Not for us, Sena. When I got to the development,
they had a sign up."

" 'Built to Scale'?"

"Yes. To *their* scale, as usual. The agent said he was
willing to let me rent if I could pay three times the tariff,
but I wouldn't."

She shrugged. "If you had agreed, there would have
been an 'unfortunate' clause in the lease, or something."
She released his hands abruptly, all the pleasure she had
taken in the morning sunlight seeping out of her. "Sam,
what are we going to do? I don't *want* to spend another
summer in a tent. Dr. Fred can afford to be patient because he's old. But we've got to live in this damned society."

"It has its drawbacks," Sam said. "But we can probably
outlive them. In the meantime, I hate to say it, but if we
don't find a house within a week or so, we'd better put in
a reservation at the Gathering Ground, just in case. There
are half a dozen new tetras released to come to Dunhill
next year, and the Society always urges them to join the
congregation even before they hit the campus." Under the
aegis of the Williamsites, many tetra social problems had
solved themselves. The enormous summer-long gathering
was made to order for tetra schedules and the sect's ideal
of "perfect religious tolerance" included tetra marriage
customs without heckling or restraints.

Sena nodded, abstractedly. Her need for a hearth and a
chimney to go with it, instead of a comradely campfire,
was the same as her desire for a ridgepole and walls instead of a tent. It was part of being human and inexorably
female. So was the ability to submerge her romantic de-
sires in a rush of practicality. "By all means, make the
reservation right away, Sam. Let's not take the chance of
being forced back into the cornfields, again."

"Oh, I don't know," he said gently. "That wasn't so
bad."

"Just the same, I keep hoping that one of these ads
will turn out to be for a lovely ramshackle old place left
over from the days when they didn't mind thinking big.
Ten-foot ceilings, and thirty-foot rooms . . . ! When you

come right down to it, a pygmy development is no good for us, even if we had the money—"

"Money," said Sam. "Well, I got the outside job I told you about—"

"I still don't quite see that. I thought we were explicitly forbidden to take any part in diploid sports, by SPEECH rules if nothing else." SPEECH was the Society for the Prevention of Exploitation of Exceptional Children, and it had loomed large for most of every tetra's young life. A trust fund and congressional backing (modelled on the state's stepping in to protect the children in an old case of multiple birth somewhere in Canada) created SPEECH: a well-intentioned, penny-pinching group of right-minded pygmies. The Society watch-dogged tetras from conception on. They checked the facilities on the chosen maternity hospital and stood by in emergencies, they contracted for and issued regular bundles of clothing perfectly suited to the climate of the individual giant child and guaranteed to be as unbecoming and institutionalized-looking as prison-stripes. Over and above the child's own family's desire to remain as inconspicuous as was compatible with a garage-sized playpen, SPEECH loomed with an endless list of 'thou shalts' and 'thou shalt nots.' Tetra children fell into blaming all their ills on the Society, and the more rigidly the Society adhered to its narrow purposes, the more justified tetra resentment became. An occasional malcontent had broken away, but it was extraordinarily difficult for a tetra to find a bushel to hide his light under; most of them simply endured their childhoods and . . . waited. . . .

Even after they departed their homes for Dunhill on the twenty-first birthday that set them technically free of the Society's octopus-like protection, they found a legal tentacle or two entwined among their adult activities. Sena, in grade school, had been barred from all games and equipment, and she was sure that the prohibition was general, forbidding all tetras at all times to engage in group sports.

"That's right," Sam said, "as far as it goes. But there's already an exhibition football team of tetras, and some exhibition teams in other sports. Strictly spectator sports: hockey, for instance, and boxing. Basketball, too. We're to play in armor, with a twenty-five-pound football, against another tetra team, and the crowds duly come in to watch us murder each other. Ought to draw pretty well."

"Sam, Sam," Sena said. She began to cry and tried to stop, furious at herself, but the slow tears would not stop rolling. The students watched, whispering interestedly. "What a beastly thing to have to do—even the ditch-digging was better—"

"Ditch-digging?" Sam said quietly. "Sena, you know what happened when I tried that. I wouldn't have quit. They fired me. And I tried to get a job as a stevedore. And a hod-carrier. And some other things of that kind. But the unions won't have it. Maybe by the time I get my doctorate there'll be a particle physicists' union, too!"

He looked abstractedly at the bright blue sky. Automatically, Sena looked up too, but there was nothing to be seen there, not even a cloud. She tried to swallow the lump in her throat, but it seemed that nothing would ever rid her of that sense of having to live every minute of her life on display, like a revolving lay figure in a second-story showwindow. If they did have to spend the summer at the Gathering Ground again, she would try to recapture that careless rapture of their first times together—but it was entirely hateful to spend their intimate coin so publicly. She could not bring herself to take his hands again in hers as a silent pledge, although that was her first impulse. The sniggering pygmies were still fascinated, watching the notoriously celibate "married" couple having a pillow-talk on the public path.

For the tetras at Dunhill, even the most harmless of the pleasures of campus life, the late-night revelations, confidences, and attempts at ordering the universe over a last beer at the corner tavern, were stringently restricted: the tetras did not fit in the booths, and had better sense than to patronize juke joints. They had to be particularly careful about drinking in public, in any event, since their enormous tolerances almost always provoked a challenge from one or another career alcoholic—a sure path to a fight, followed inevitably by a riot. Their most intimate conversations always seemed to be carried on in the middle of a sidewalk in broad daylight.

Sam seldom seemed to mind. His attitude was that the situation was certainly unpleasant, but not intolerable, since much of the talk was—literally—over the diploids' heads. At least, he could point out, tetras were seldom spied upon in lovers' lanes any more: in such darkness and

isolation several diploids had gone looking for easy amusement, forgetting the acuteness of tetra eyes and ears. A
few broken bones, underlined by bruises and contusions,
had put an end to the practice.

"But they're right, by their own lights," he said at last.
"Where muscles still count, we're labor-saving machines.
We can do more heavy work, and do it faster, than the
diploids can. If the unions admitted us, sooner or later the
diploids would be out of work. But this exhibition football
team doesn't do any economic harm to the diploids, because we aren't allowed to play against any but our own
kind. Do you know what Methfessel—that's the promoter
—wants to do next?"

"What?" Sena said in a small voice.

"He wants to stage tournaments. The real thing; he
wants to put tetras on big brewery Percherons, give them
spears, swords, all the rest of the medieval armory. If he
can get police approval, he'll pay up to a hundred bucks
a day."

"For murder!"

"Not necessarily. Maurey says molybdenum steel would
make a strong enough armor against a light spear, aluminum for instance, or even dural. And of course swords
would be just a joke—"

"Sam, don't you see? They're making us fight each other!
How long would it be before we began to take these tournaments seriously? Before we split up into rival groups
like the Roman charioteers, with betting, bribes, assassina-
tions and all the rest? Maurey must be mad even to consider it!"

"Well, Maurey's pretty bright," Sam said neutrally.
"Anyhow I'm not in on the tournament deal, Sena. I'm
just playing this armor-plated football. It's rough, but it's
extra income for us. Maybe we'll find ourselves that house
after a while."

"Maybe," Sena said. She had herself back under control, more or less. They linked arms and began to stroll
toward their next scheduled class. The students, disap-
pointed, began to trickle away. "In the meantime we'll just
have to go on living in the dormitories, I suppose. I envy
people like you and Kelland, with parents living near the
University. That must make it easier."

"It doesn't," Sam said, with some surprise. "I don't

know how it is with Kelland, but my folks are afraid of me; they wouldn't let you see it, but it's the truth. Somehow they thought the paracolchicine treatment was just a sort of health tonic. They didn't understand ten per cent of Dr. Fred's explanation, they just thought tetraploidy was a sort of guarantee that I'd turn out big and strong. Now it's 'oh, not so *damned* shaggy!' You know how that goes. I think perhaps they expected the subsidy from the Society to be extra income, too, instead of being all used up for the big beds and the special dungarees and all the testing routines. And my older brother hates my guts. I make him feel puny—and he still claims it hurts his business connections to have a tetra in the family. He made it sound like my father kept a live crocodile on a leash—until good old SPEECH stopped paying the bills."

"I know," Sena said somberly. "But Sam, it's worth it. We've got to believe that—otherwise, where are we?"

"Where, then?" Sam said. "I wish I knew."

"There's an old Indian legend about the horned devil caterpillar," Sena said. "Ernest Seton-Thompson tells about it in one of his books. Mother Carey offered the devil a drink from the Double Cup. One half held wine, and the other half held, I forget, something unpleasant; anyhow there was only one place to drink, so you got a little of each. That was how the horned devil got to be so ugly as a caterpillar, and so beautiful as a butterfly."

Sam snorted vigorously, though his eyes were tender.

"I know that business," he said, "that's just pie-in-the-sky—the old Emersonian compensation. I'm out to make things better for us poor damned caterpillars. You don't soothe me by promising me that I'll be a pretty butterfly in the sweet by-and-by. That's a diploid bill of goods."

"All right," Sena said. "I don't believe it either. But all the same, it's something to think about."

"Maybe," Sam said.

Sena's long stride matched his, but what she said was: "Sam, I'm going to spend this weekend with Polly. I want to pretend I'm a butterfly. It does something for me to sit in an armchair that makes me feel delicate and feminine."

"And enthroned?"

"I said pretend, Sam! She paid too high a price for what she's got, but I don't have to pay a thing."

He thought about reminding her that no other tetra

woman would consider it worth the risk. Tetras mentioned Polly, if at all, in terms of loathing. Sena had befriended the headstrong beauty in little girlhood, however, and was her only friend since the respectable marriage that had, paradoxically, ruined her. She did not waste her breath defending Polly, or Polly's built-to-her-scale wing of the Boyston mansion. Instead, Sena went openly to visit the tetras' only black sheep, and Sam had sometimes found himself wondering a little why.

"Well," he said slowly, "as long as I can be sure of that—" He sighed. "You're very loyal, Sena!"

"Don't admire me, Sam! It isn't only her armchairs, you know. Do you realize that hers is the only bathtub in the world I can stretch out in and really be luxurious?"

They clung together, laughing, when he said superciliously, "I'm a shower man myself. Me and all the other tetras."

—Making a virtue of having to stand all hunched over in the shower stall. Some of us routinely get down on our knees to get clean. Will there ever be room enough for us to flex our muscles without actually making a fist?

To that suddenly wordless communion, Sena added: The sweet privacy of love, and doorways to stride through together.

They stooped instinctively to enter the Humanities Building, although, as it happened, the archway was quite high enough to have accommodated them.

The university chapel's carillon began to chime; it was playing Bortnianski's *Ich bete an die Macht der Liebe.* "Hey, just in time," Sam said. "We were almost late for Philosophy."

II

The puppy was now five weeks old. She was able to stagger about the laboratory floor, and to essay a tentative bounce or two, but she was given to frequent collapses of the rear section, and unexpected subsidences into sleep in the middle of some grandiose project. She had a bed of her own, but preferred to sleep in the overturned wastebasket, which was far too small for her.

Dr. Fred—Frederick R. Hyatt, Sc. D., on formal days—looked at her critically while she chewed on a leg of his desk. Maurice St. George watched them both, with an expression which seemed to indicate that he didn't know which of the two amused him more.

"But why a dog, Dr. Fred?" he said. "Surely you must have finished all the experimenting with animals before you asked for human volunteers. Something new?"

"Hmm?" Dr. Fred said. "New? No, not very. It's a line I abandoned temporarily in the early stages of high mammals—dogs, cats, and so on—have short childhoods and long adult lives, except man himself. I was wondering just what that had to do with chromosome parity. So I tried it with her. She's a test-tube baby; her mother was artificially inseminated, with spermatozoa in physiological salt solution plus a dollop of paracolchicine and a little DNA —desoxyribonucleic acid. The ovum wasn't treated."

"Only the sperm chromosomes doubled, then?" Maurey said.

"That's right," Dr. Fred said. "She's a triploid, not a tetraploid. Looks like she's going to be a horse, though, just like the rest of my children. And she's retarded for her age. I'd been hoping for that, but I hadn't really expected it."

The puppy toppled over, blamed Maurey for it, spread her legs to do battle, and released a deafening yap of exasperation. Dr. Fred heaved her up and put her back in her box, throwing the dog-hairy blanket over her head.

"Go to sleep, Decibelle."

Finding it suddenly dark, Decibelle grumbled and obediently—if involuntarily—fell asleep.

"She'll make a fine pet," Maurey said.

"Don't you believe it, Maurice. We don't dare spring gigantic animals on the public at this stage of the game. She's going to be the world's biggest mutt—bigger than any possible Great Dane or St. Bernard. We'd have an injunction slapped on us at once. You know how constantly the diploids grub after that kind of opening."

Maurey stood up. Dr. Fred noted interestedly that he did not duck his head as he did so, a gesture that was habitual with the other tetraploids. Of course the normal room ceiling offered ample clearance for even the tallest of them, but the *feeling* of being boxed in was hard to battle. Maurey, evidently, had conquered it. He seemed generally to be the best adjusted to his status of all the giants; and inarguably he had the highest IQ.

Well, no reason to be surprised at that. Despite its inducing of doubling in the chromosomes—or, more accurately, its inhibition of reduction-division during mitosis—the paracolchicine treatment did not really have any genetic effect; that is, it did not affect the genes themselves. What it produced was called a "mutation" because it was a change of form which, once fixed by DNA, bred true. But it was not a true mutation, a cataclysmic mutation springing directly from chemical change in the heterochromatin of the genes. Instead, it simply made it possible for the ultimate somatic expression of the individual's inheritance to come through on a tremendous scale. If there were brains in that great dark head, it was none of Dr. Fred's doing.

Still, high intelligence did not imply superior ability to come to terms with one's social environment; indeed, there seemed to be some sort of rough correlation between high intelligence and the accumulation of aberrations. That was part of the price one paid for a society which put a premium on mediocrity, and there was no way one could choose not to pay it—changing the society was a job for generations, and in the meantime one had to survive somehow. There wasn't a tetra alive who hadn't had a crush-ingly difficult childhood, most of them in total isolation from their peers.

Dr. Fred sighed inaudibly. The pioneering experiments in polyploidy hadn't had such bafflingly complex overtones; neither chickweed nor rabbits are much bothered by emotional upsets. He wanted badly to know the nature of Maurey's adjustment, but he was not a psychologist and had no training in that field, and a lively sense of the personal inviolability of his "children" would not allow him to require them to submit to analysis. In the decade and a little more since the second batch had reached adulthood and been released from the "protection" of the Society for the Prevention of Exploitation of Exceptional Children, he had offered to take them all, without exception, under his wing. Most of them had settled in willingly enough; a very few had chosen the wide, wide world instead of Dunhill.

Through the grimy window of the lab he saw Sena and Sam, talking earnestly on the sidewalk near the building. They all *were* children, really, very alone in a settled world, and still prone to whisperings, gigglings and secret societies with long names. Except that their elders might yet kill them for that secrecy—or for less understandable reasons.

"I'd like to have that dog," Maurey said, thrusting his hands into his jacket pockets. "I don't think I'd be afraid of the diploid neighbors."

"Sorry, Maurice. Not yet. I need her here, anyhow."

"I grant that you need her, since she's triploid," Maurey said. He looked down at the huddled blanket, frowning. "But I want her when you're through. No matter how big she becomes, the law can't fit an ordinary dog into the description of a wild animal being kept *res naturae*, and there's no other way they could take her from me unless she gets rabid or something like that."

Dr. Fred forked his fingers and pushed his glasses up against his eyebrows. They were old glasses—for his eyesight had stabilized years ago—with battered mother-of-pearl nosepieces, and every time he had to look down at the puppy they slid solemnly down to the end of his nose. He had been putting off having them adjusted, and now he knew he never would, for the oculist would need only one look into his eyes to see the destructive changes being brought about in his retinas by his hypertension; and Dr. Fred had a strong instinct for symbols. The first pair of glasses prescribed for him for *that* reason would be his concession that Death was nearby.

"You'll just make trouble," he said. "I've no doubt you could beat the law on such a matter, Maurice, but I don't think it advisable to try. It isn't the laws that exist now that we have to worry about, but the laws the diploids will enact later if we give them cause."

"Forgive me, Dr. Fred, but I think you're overcautious. And perhaps overly modest, too. The giants are here to stay, and there's no point in continuing this crawfishing way from conflict with the diploids. There are plenty of provable advantages to tetraploid animals. Cats, for instance. A tetraploid cat would be the perfect answer to the rat problem. Five times out of ten, a diploid cat won't mess with a rat at all."

"Cats," Dr. Fred said, "have a way of lying down, grabbing with their front legs, and kicking with their hind feet when they feel playful. A tetraploid cat that did that with a diploid child would rip the child to shreds."

"Such a cat would be no more dangerous to the human child than the bathtub, statistically."

"Maurice, you aren't dealing with statistics. You're dealing with emotions. The fifteen tetras in Pasadena had logic and reason on their side. Have you forgotten what happened to them?"

His hands still dug into his coat pockets, Maurey turned on his heel, took three quick steps, and struck the crown of his head violently against the door lintel. Dr. Fred winced in sympathy. Maurey stood stilently, his back to the room; evidently his bolt for the door had been a "wild" impulse which, once arrested, he was able to consider. Then he turned.

"No, I haven't forgotten," he said. His eyes were streaming tears, but he wore a twisted, triumphant smile, as if his failure to swear at his accident, or his aborted flight, were a major victory. "I won't ever forget that. The diploids are trying to forget that it ever happened, but I won't ever forget. They weren't very bright, those fifteen; we've learned from them. They depended on force alone, not logic—just force. They forgot force's necessary adjunct."

"And what is that, please?"

"Fraud," Maurey said. He went out.

Dr. Fred watched him go, blinking unhappily. Maybe Maurey's "adjustment" was—

The puppy grumbled and thrust her head up out of the blanket. Dr. Fred pushed her nose back down into a corner of the box.

"Sleep, dammit."

III

The Titans, as Ira Methfessel had dubbed his first team, followed the practice plays obediently enough, but even without the armor they were slow—almost as slow in their heads as they were with their feet. Most of the young tetraploids had seen plenty of football games, having spent most of their lives to date on the University campus, but they had never been allowed to play during their undergraduate days; and the armor and the business of managing the shoulder jets was a double handicap.

After the first blackboard session, Ira disgustedly cut down the plays to four or five cross-bucks, two rudimentary spinners, and a few laterals—all, in essense, straight power plays. It seemed to console him somewhat to meditate that the opposing team, the Atlanteans, were tetras too, and unlikely to be any better than the Titans; and, anyhow, all the crowd wanted was the kick of so much brute force in combat.

Ira was a diploid, the only one on the team; they had all been surprised when the promoter had insisted on playing with them, but there was no doubt that he was good at it. He was nearly seven feet high, with flaming red hair, but he looked like a freshman among the hulking tetras. Nevertheless he treated them like high school kids. He sweated and swore, and the giants swore back cheerfully, got in each other's way, dropped the weighted, jet-powered football, and moved their big feet a little faster. By the day of the game, Ira had whipped his bulky charges into something that resembled a flexible and resourceful team instead of a herd of rhinoceroses.

It showed results almost at once. The first ball jammed somehow at kickoff and went completely out of the stadium, still under power—it was picked up later outside of town, partially melted—but Sam got the next one and made off with it. The Titans made their first down with a clangor like a chorus of trip-hammers.

"Good," Ira told the huddle. "Sam, try not to use the jets so much. If you call on them during a scrimmage you'll hit somebody and we'll be penalized."

"Okay," Sam said. "I was trying to get clear of that left guard of theirs—"

"Sure; but you're not allowed to hit a man while you're under power, you know that. Lucky the ref didn't see it, even though it was an accident. All right, number eighty this time."

The Titans fanned out, the bright armor glittering and flashing in the sunlight, and crouched along the rush line. Sam took his left half spot and hunched watchfully. He was surprised to find that he was enjoying himself. The emotions of that first brutal striving, the clashing of mailed shoulders and chests, the pistoning of sollerets against the rubbery turf, released in him a willingness to hate that thirty years of Dr. Fred's indoctrination had not been able quite to quell.

Hammy Saunders fired the aluminum ball back, its stripes of black and yellow paint turning lazily as it travelled; it looked like an obese hornet. Ira snaffled it and pitched it underhand to Sam. Already the armored figures were deploying, fending off their opponents with battering gauntlets. The crowd howled delightedly.

Sam located Hammy's red-splashed pauldrons among the scattering giants and pulled the ball back. His latticed plastic helmet was beginning to fog. An Atlantean bore down at him from the right.

He fired the ball. It soared, riding the thin, hazy flame of its plasma jet. Hammy faded back, his shoulder-jets spitting, and left the turf in a tremendous leap. The ball slammed into his chest under full acceleration. He somersaulted once and hit the ground.

He stayed there.

The ref's whistle blew. The two teams milled and converged, rivalry forgotten. Sam wormed his way into the melee.

Hammy's helmet had spit along the line of the front lattice. A dinged-in bar had dug out his right eye, which lay next to his ear, free upon the cable of its nerve-trunk.

Blood swamped the entire side of his head. He was still clinging to the ball. The grandstands yelled their approval.

"Look out, Sam," Ira's voice said. "Cripes, let a man through, you guys, can't you? He needs hospitalization—break it up, break it up—"

The giants, on both sides, made a low and ugly growling. The refs separated them hurriedly. Hammy was taken off on a stretcher.

Sam, don't you see? They're making us fight each other!

In the huddle, Ira said:

"Let's get back at 'em. They can't get away with that kind of stuff. Let's murder the bastards. Take a straight buck across left guard—that guy hasn't had a fist in his face yet—"

"Not me," Sam said.

"Eh? Don't give me that, Ettinger. Who's running this show?"

"You are," Sam said. "But I'm quitting. The Atlanteans didn't do anything to Hammy. It was an accident. He lost his eye because he was playing this damn fool game. I'm quitting."

"You're yellow, you lummox."

Sam reached out with one ring-mailed gauntlet and took Ira by his left shoulder. The tough metal bent in his grip. The diploid stumbled, flailing for balance.

"Leggo, you—"

"Be careful of your language, squirt," Sam said. He swallowed. His eyes burned in their sockets, and the armor creaked across his shoulders. "I'm sick of your games. For two cents I'd take you apart."

He jerked his hand away suddenly. The pauldron came away with it, with a screech of outraged metal. Sam took it in both hands and crumpled it methodically, like pasteboard. The sudden, irregular *give* of the plate in his palms was like the breaking of bone, and he was shaken by an ugly love for it.

"Here," he said. He handed the wadded plating back to the promoter, his mouth twitching with the bitterness in it. "Be glad it wasn't you. I'm quitting. Quitting—*now* do you understand?"

Ira took the bunched mail numbly, staring at Sam through his slotted plastic fishbowl.

"Look, Sam," he said. "You're blaming me for this. I

didn't do it. Nobody did it, just like you say. You knew this job was dangerous, and so did Hammy—"

The ref's whistle screamed, and the whole tense group was marched five yards down the field for overtime. None of the Titans seemed to notice; they followed the quarrel and gathered around it again. Some of the Atlanteans began to filter over into the Titan huddle.

Baffled, the refs blew time out, though nobody had asked for it yet. The crowd grumbled with puzzled impatience.

"Ira's right," Chris Harper said. "It wasn't his fault."

"I said I knew it was an accident," Sam growled. "Just the kind of accident the shrimps in the stands came to see. That's the penalty we pay for being so numerous—if there were fewer of us, we could make our livings in sideshows. I'm through with both kinds."

He strode off the field, his pads creaking. The crowd booed him enthusiastically.

Maurey was waiting for him as he came out of the locker room. The older giant was wearing a crooked smile that puzzled Sam, and, in his present mood, infuriated him despite his respect for his chief.

"What are you grinning at, Maurey?" he demanded. "You think it's funny when a man loses an eye—like them —back there?" He jerked a thumb over his shoulder in the direction of the bleachers.

"Not at all," Maurey said soothingly. The crooked smile dimmed a little, but did not quite disappear. "I take it pretty seriously, I assure you, Sam. Going back to the lab?"

"Yes—if you need me. In fact I might as well, anyhow. I've got no place else to go until Sena is free."

"Good," Maurey said. "I'll give you a lift, if you like. My roader's in the parking lot."

That was odd; Maurey had never shown any interest in sports. But of course most of the tetras had asked his advice when the problem of the exhibition teams had first come up; he had probably come to see whether or not he had been wrong in recommending the project. Sam wondered what he was thinking now.

Maurey, however, said nothing further until the road-plane was on the express lane leading back toward town, trailing its stubby wings; and even then he seemed only to be making talk. Finally he touched the switch that pulled the wings into place and snapped the rotor open, turned the craft up a ski-jump, and climbed steeply.

At 4,000 feet he said:

"So Ira's finally made you mad."

"Yeah," Sam said. The word was muffled. He sat immobile, staring straight ahead. He had already begun to feel a little guilty for his outburst on the field, but Maurey's question made him feel rebellious all over again. "I think maybe it's about time this damned culture found productive jobs for us, Maurey. We can't all be graduate assistants all our lives—or professors, for that matter. There are lots of us like Hammy, who haven't got the academic temperament."

"And Hammy's first outside job didn't do him much good."

"That's one way of putting it. But the accident wasn't Ira's fault. It was the fault of all diploids."

"All?" Maurey said quietly.

"Yes, all. I suppose you want me to except Dr. Fred. Well, I won't. He means well. But he's been one of the major factors in keeping us satisfied—moderately, anyhow —with the status quo. That can't last forever."

Maurey cast a sidelong glance at him, instinctively banking the roader to the right so as to be able to see the ground past Sam; he was a born pilot.

"I've been telling Dr. Fred exactly that," he said, looking away and swinging back left. "But he's too old to change. We'll have to make our future ourselves, if it's to suit us when we get it."

"You've something in mind?" Sam said curiously.

"Yes, I think so. I want to be sure I'm not just setting up a Pasadena before I talk too much about it, though."

"I'm a quiet sort," Sam said. "Can't you give me some idea—"

"Well, in essence it's quite simple. I want to start a homesteading project. The unmilitarized part of the Moon has just been declared public land. I think we could occupy it profitably."

"That sounds unlikely," Sam said. "What would we do for a living?"

"Farm bacteria."

"Maurey, *I* know you're not crazy, but you're going to

have to explain if you expect me to understand. I don't know what the hell you're talking about."

Maurey grinned. "There's no air on the Moon, Sam. We could use the sewage from the Army base as a soil, and grow anaerobic bacteria right out in fields. There's a market for them, for serums, anti-toxins and so on. Tetanus, gas gangrene, all the obligate anaerobes. And then there's the cancer problem; the cancer cell is a fermentation-based anaerobe; we could raise them on an unprecedented scale, for research. A genetics laboratory would go along with it, since we'd be getting new mutations constantly, with all that hard radiation around; some of the new strains might produce useful antibiotics, or who-knows-what? It would be practical, believe me—I've studied it."

"All right," Sam said. "Anyhow it *is* Pasadena all over again, Maurey, and it's just what the diploids would like— get us all into a ghetto somewhere where they could bomb us to extinction all at once."

Maurey peered downward, and then began to sidle the roader toward the Earth.

"I'm not quite so stupid, Sam," he said, smiling again. "Of course it's like the Pasadena thing on the surface— intentionally. I made up my mind long ago that the only way to get anything from the diploids is to seem to be doing things their way. *Seem* to be, Sam. Actually I think our lunar tetraploid homeland wouldn't last more than a year or so. By the end of that time we'll either be extinct, or be in a position to dictate the terms of our tenancy on diploid Earth. I hope that some day we can have a *real* planet, and I rather hope it'll be this one; the tetras are bound to multiply. Most parents will become more and more reluctant to deny their children the advantage of tetraploidy in a world where tetras are part of the normal order of things."

Sam was a little confused.

"You forget the low-fertility angle," he objected. "There's still plenty of religious and moralistic opposition to our serial-marriage arrangements—and even more sentimental worship of motherhood. Many a family would drop dead before it would make a prospective daughter into a giantess—that's why we're so short of women—and the diploids are already too proud of being more fertile than we are."

"Sure, sure. That's as may be. I didn't say this was going to be easy. Ever heard of the Taylor Grazing Act? It requires that a homesteader personally inspect the land he's filed for, and certify that it's more suitable for farming than for any other purpose. That's not going to be easy on the Moon."

Maurey dropped the roader skillfully to the highway, collapsed the wings and rotor, and guided it to the lane that led to the university.

"My point," he said, "is that we'll have to seem to be playing along with the diploids for a while. In the final analysis, our job is just this: to trick the diploids into putting weapons into our hands. Maybe the Moon isn't one of them, maybe it is. Dr. Fred has already given us one—"

"You mean size? That's not—"

"No, that's no great advantage yet. And besides, it's not the *kind* of weapon I mean. Have you met Decibelle?"

"That fool puppy? You bet. She mangles my shoelaces."

"That dog is a time-bomb," Maurey said, with intense seriousness. "Dr. Fred doesn't see all the implications, I'm glad to say. Or take our own lab work. The reactionless effect we've got on the bench right now will be a weapon sooner or later. We have you to thank for that, Sam. *Any-thing* is a weapon if you know which end is the business end. Right now, I'm depending most of all upon Ira and his silly tournament."

"Great God," Sam said. "The next thing you'll be saying is that you want me to go back and play football for Ira again."

"I want you to do exactly that," Maurey said calmly. "I can't order you to do it, because I'm your superior only in the lab—but I'd appreciate it if you would. I want Ira's tournament promoted for all it's worth. If we can get the reactionless effect developed in time, I'm going to give that to Ira, too; it'll be a great improvement over those shoulder-jets, and a hell of a lot less dangerous. Or more dangerous, depending on how we want to use it—as a weapon, it could be one of the deadliest side-arms in history—among other things. I leave it to you, Sam, to imagine what those other things might be. Here we are."

He garaged the roadplane in the radiation lab's basement and swung the door open.

"Coming up?"

"Sure." Sam said abstractedly. "What's the great to-do about the reactionless effect, Maurey? It's only a laboratory toy as far as I can see. I'm pretty well convinced that we'll find out where the backlash is going to, before long."

"We haven't found it yet."

"No-o-o-o. But I still think it must be getting recirculated somewhere, somehow, the way a regenerative circuit uses back E.M.F. Otherwise it'd show up as an entropy loss. It isn't possible that there should be no reaction at all."

Maurey shrugged. "Mr. Newton's Third Law of Motion may not be any more universal than any of his other laws," he said. "By all means keep trying to find where the recoil is going, so there'll be no mistake before we publish. But if it turns out that there *isn't* any 'equal and opposite effect'—"

"There will be," Sam said flatly. "There always is. Aren't you coming up too, Maurey?"

"No, I've got work elsewhere. You have your key, haven't you? All right—see you tomorrow."

"Thanks for the lift."

"My pleasure. Think about what I said."

Sam climbed the stairs and let himself into the barn-like radiation lab. He had hardly been aware of Maurey's departure. Essentially a scientist, Sam was easily swayed when it came to political maneuvering—but the faintest smell of a technical puzzle was enough to wipe politics from his mind. He had already forgotten the quarrel with Methfessel; he had almost forgotten Maurey's hints about a tetraploid "homeland." The outrageous suggestion that Newton's Third Law of Motion actually might not apply to his toy had been enough to enlist his total attention.

He plugged the power jacks into the apparatus and waited for the tubes to warm up. That waste of power, made necessary by the impossibility of using transistors throughout the apparatus, he understood; but this other imbalance—

The experiment, originally, had been set up to explore some side effects of superconductivity in the solid state; a routine job, being handled by Maurey on commission for the federal high-altitude project—the authority having jurisdiction over the orbital platform, SV-1. Maurey and Sam had guessed that the government hoped to perfect some radical principles in operating electronic circuits raw, in the near-vacuum of space, utilizing the constant wash of charged particles available out there. Thus far, however, nothing along that line had appeared; instead—

He touched the key experimentally. Across the room a large bell chimed pleasantly, though it was not in any way connected with the apparatus. Sam got up, took down the bell, and put up the regular target, which was metered.

The machine was behaving as always. Every erg of energy that went into it was monitored; even the losses in metering were figured in, right down to the corrections for entropy. And the amount of thrust that that invisible pulse shot at the target always equalled exactly the amount of power that the apparatus used.

There was no equivalent "recoil."

Suppose that that apparent lack of response was real, as Maurey had suggested? Suppose that, for once, an action did *not* involve an equal and opposite reaction? Suppose that, just this once, an object that was pushed *didn't push back?*

Of course, the target pushed back, but that was second-ary—*ex post facto*, as it were. He changed the metering setup and started again. There was no gain in the amount of energy put out by the heaters in the tubes when the device was "fired." The chassis wiring didn't heat up, either. Suddenly, he remembered that superconductivity was, after all, supposed to have something to do with all this; if the wiring didn't heat at room temperature, what would happen if the whole shebang were supercooled?

He had no way of accomplishing that today; but he was able to make a free coil of the main power pack lead, made a foray next door to liberate a beaker of liquid air from the pressure lab, and dipped the coil in that.

The target burst the moment the key was closed. Excitedly Sam checked the target meter readings against the lowered resistance of the cold coil. It checked to the last decimal place. Nothing lost in resistance, then? The boiling of the liquid air hadn't speeded visibly when the pulse was launched, but the eye couldn't be trusted to detect that kind of effect. As a last check, he bottled the liquid air and the coil in a Dewar flask with a sensitive Sostman transducer for a cork; the transducer was already wired into its own Honeywell recording system.

He fired the device four times. The steadily rising line on the Honeywell chart showed not the slightest joggle from bottom to top: the pressure rose as the liquid air boiled, but the passage of energy through the coil didn't speed it any. And yet supercooling the coil *had* allowed more current to get through. No need now to worry about radio or suboptical effects which might be invisibly taking power off; this test was enough to make any professor of thermodynamics become a Rosicrucian instead. In fact—

Newton's Third Law of Motion was repealed. He felt obscurely that Maurey had magicked it out of existence. A math to delimit the effect could wait; as a matter of fact it would be fairly easy to express it as a matrix discontinuity on the level of mechanics, though accounting for it thermodynamically would not be so simple. What interested Sam now was a thoroughly practical piece of gadgeteering: finding a way for re-assembling the breadboard rig so that it would be portable. Even to his untrained engineering eye, the advantages of portability were evident.

If a man could hold a thing like this in his hand, and apply just as much push to an object as there was power available—if he could, for instance, convert a couple of thousand kilowatts into physical thrust against a heavy load—then a lot of heavy machinery was going to become obsolete very suddenly. Consider a derailed locomotive in a culvert; four men with such portable devices could tie them into the nearest high-tension line and lever the locomotive back onto the tracks without any effort, and without bothering to call for a crane.

The engineering of a compact projector did not prove to be difficult. All but two of the tubes could be replaced by two acorn 6AL6s without much loss in efficiency (in the unique sense in which the concept of "efficiency" could be said to apply here at all), and the loss could be expressed as heat and dissipated harmlessly by discharging the pulse from a flanged tube with a reflector behind it. The flanging might be charged, too, to make a focussing field, and the tube could be silver and act as a wave-guide so that very little power would actually be needed to keep the beam tight—

In another hour, Sam had a thing that might have been a twenty-first century crossbow, without the bow. It was certainly awkward, but it worked. Sam sat in a window of the radiation lab and knocked off the hats of passersby until dusk made aiming too difficult. It did not occur to Sam that until it got a little darker still, he might very well have continued with the sport so long as he did not care whether it was the passersby's hats or their heads he knocked off.

Whistling tunelessly, Sam locked up and went back to the dorms.

The last of Roger Bacon's engineering dreams, that of a machine to raise and lower heavy weights which might be held in one hand, had been realized. It had taken eight centuries.

A student of history might have known where to look for the missing "equal and opposite reaction"; but Sam was only a scientist.

IV

The windows of the graduate lab in radiation were like the windows of every other laboratory in the ancient University—big, inadequately puttied, and too infrequently washed. Maurey did not see the device on the bench until he had been in the lab for several minutes, for the sunlight was slanted the other way, and the side workbench was only dimly lit in the morning this time of year. It got direct sunlight only from about noon to 2:00 p.m.

When he did see the gadget, he drew in his breath sharply. It took only a moment to check the schematic, and to confirm that this was what had been yesterday only a confusion of tubes and tangles of wire. Maurey looked it over with almost microscopic care after that.

What he saw raised his estimate of Sam, already high in this department, by quite a few notches. Yesterday the generator of the one-way push had taken up as much space as an ancient superheterodyne radio. Now it was all neatly assembled along a single axis, and was scarcely more difficult to handle than a shotgun except for the trailing tether of the input lead.

Sam had given Maurey his weapon.

Maurey shut the door quietly and locked it. He had an undergraduate due for a conference, but let him find the door locked—it would be the first time that Maurey had ever missed such an engagement, so it would never occur to the student that Maurey had locked the door against him. This was more important (though he would have to be careful never to break a date with a tutorial charge again; the undergraduates were important too: they were potentially useful).

The discarded, empty, bone-dry Dewar flask told its own story. It also suggested something that Sam evidently had overlooked. Maurey traced down Sam's free coil and made a receptacle for it, by providing clips to hold the Dewar flask under the silver barrel of the gun. He got his liquid air from the same source that Sam had; but instead of corking the flask, he soldered a conduit from it to a tiny, fan-driven booster-generator. Two flashlight batteries and a miniaturized transformer—to serve as a power source for the trigger, nothing else—finished the job; he cast the input lead free.

The device was completely portable now, and would deliver a considerable thrust—without any counterthrust—as long as the liquid air held out. In a heavy-duty, semi-portable projector, some of the output could be diverted to run a compressor which would keep replenishing the liquid air.

And *that* would upset more than the Third Law of Motion. It would also eradicate the Second Law of Thermodynamics from the books; for such a device would be the world's first genuine perpetual motion machine, which the Second Law says is impossible. The prospect rather dazed even Maurey.

Somebody knocked. Maurey sat quietly until he could hear his visitor going away. Then he left, taking the projector with him, bundled into an innocuous lump in old newspapers.

On the campus, students waved to him—even diploids. Maurey was well liked. His air of mild, cosmopolitan amusement made him envied by the young (and suspected of homosexuality or radicalism by the old); and among the students there was an idealistic "equal rights for tetras" movement which Maurey had taken great care to further. The diploid kids loved Maurey, where they only respected the younger giants.

"Hi, Maurey, Whatcha got?"

"Wet-pack," Maurey said. He had picked this term up from a biologist colleague in the faculty dining hall; he had no idea what it was, but it sounded perishable—that was all he cared about now. "How are you, June? Get over that squabble with the parents all right?"

"Yes, thanks to you. Are you coming to our meeting tonight?"

"I hope so. Don't wait up for me, though."

He tucked a flap of newspaper back over the weapon, nodded to the girl, and turned down the gravel path past the old green statue of Charles S. Peirce expounding philosophy from his chair, as he was said to have done one year at the University in the dim past. At the other end of the campus he saw another giant, but the distance was too great to see who it was. It was male, and that was all Maurey could determine.

He had a sudden urge to run shouting toward the towering figure, to declare war at once upon all the scurrying pygmies, pick them off like clay pigeons with the invincible thing he had wrapped in ancient history under his arm—

No. Not yet. He went on, smiling to the diploid youngsters who worshipped him.

He realized that his own immediate plan was far from perfect. The most important thing had been to get the weapon out of the radiology lab, and out of the Physics Building entirely. There the chances were good that anyone who ran across it might understand it—or understand enough about it to become dangerously curious.

Sam wouldn't trouble himself too much about its disappearance. He would assume that Maurey had taken it, and as soon as he found that assumption to be true he would be satisfied. Dr. Fred, on the other hand, would "know" immediately that the thing was not a weapon, but some toy of the radiology labs; so probably the best place for it was in Dr. Fred's safe, at least until it could be delivered to Methfessel. Dr. Fred was almost fanatical about respecting the property rights, both material and intellectual, of the giants. When he found the projector he would identify it as Maurey's and leave it alone.

All this was parlor psychology, based insecurely upon Maurey's estimate of the people involved, but it would have to do. The most important job now was to persuade Sam not to publish his findings. It would take some doing, for Sam, even more than the ordinary instructor-cum-graduate-assistant, depended upon his scientific reputation for his small income. A discovery as revolutionary as this might net him an assistant professorship—or even an independent government development contract, which would take him out from under Maurey's invisible control entirely.

But he was not out from under yet. Maurey did not really think he ever would make it—not, at least, until it didn't matter to Maurey any more.

Maurey was mildly surprised to find Dr. Fred's lab empty. The old man rarely went out these days. He held the rank of professor emeritus, hence had no classes to teach except those he chose to teach, which were few and irregular. He spent most of his waking hours (which meant twenty out of every twenty-four) making microtome sections, fixing, staining, mounting, sketching, and filing the thousands of tissue specimens necessary to any experiment in polyploidy. Lately the tempo of this work had increased markedly; Dr. Fred, Maurey knew, was getting the last possible moment of good out of his failing eyesight, before the retinal destruction rendered useless the rest of his fabulous skills and techniques.

Evidently he was now taking one of his unpredictable four-hour naps. Well, perhaps that was all to the good; it meant less to explain. Like all really gifted liars, Maurey begrudged himself every lie he told, for he knew well that lying is a miniaturist's art—practised on a large scale it becomes vulgar, and eventually unviable.

Maurey knelt before the safe. One of the sloppy human abilities tetraploidy had sharpened for Maurey was hearing: the muscles of his middle ear were as sensitive as those of the pupils of his eyes, and could reduce the vibrating surface of his eardrum to a taut spot no bigger than a pinhead when he was listening intently for tuned sounds. He could hear from four cycles per second to 30,000, and do it selectively; if he wished, he could filter a single pure tone out of the most outrageous hash of background noise; it was his theory—though he had never been in an enclosure quiet enough to test it, and doubted that he ever would—that he should be able to hear the impact of a single molecule against his tympanum. His mind had recorded the tiny tinkle of tumblers almost automatically, the first time Dr. Fred had opened that safe.

The door swung open, and Maurey sniffed with annoyance. Here was a problem he hadn't anticipated. The safe was full of papers. More than full; it was stuffed. Two of the three top pigeonholes were taken up by slide-boxes, the third by the familiar cardboard mailing tubes in which paracolchicine ampules came into the lab from Columbian Pharmaceuticals, the huge plant just across the river from the University. The rest of the safe was packed with notepaper, graph-paper, drawing-paper, photomicrographs, letters, thin pamphlets with long titles, file cards, and what seemed to be at least a thousand shiny black booklets of silicone-treated lens-cleaning paper. A sizeable proportion of the mess sagged chummily into Maurey's lap the moment the safe door moved back.

He swore. From a box under the table something sneezed in answer, and Decibelle stuck her nose out and regarded Maurey with reproachful brown eyes, her eyebrows going up and down independently.

"Go to sleep, pooch. Damn! What am I going to do with this—"

He realized that he was talking to himself, not to the dog, and stopped. As a preliminary measure, he took all the papers out of the safe and made four piles of them on the workbench. Obviously the stuff had been jammed into the safe in no particular order, so it would do no harm to redistribute it in some way which would be more economical of space. Probably the best way would be to stack according to size, all of the films in one pile, all the notes in another, the publications in another, and so on, and then repack—

Maurey's hand, turning over a crumpled letter-size sheet, paused in mid-air. After a long moment it continued the arrested motion, laying the sheet with meticulous care upon the proper pile. Maurey picked up the sheet that had been under it and read it with fierce concentration.

CARLIN, SENA HYATT

(Jane Hyatt
(Anthony Armisted Carlin

Series 0-573-9-002
Sex-linked double-diploid with marked tetraploidy; cf. chromosome charts 2, 3, 6, 8, 9, 10, 14, 15, 18, 21, 22, 24. Heavy crossing-over on diploid chromosomes. Triploid x-chromosome; cytological sex female. Somatically an apparently normal tetraploid individual with only slight schisming after RNA injections at adulthood. No DNA shift planned, this being emergent stock . . .

It was no news, of course, that Sena had Hyatt blood in her. Most of the older giants did; only the youngest generation had had to suffer from the court order forbidding Dr. Fred and his half-sister to contribute germ cells to the polyploidy experiments—an order stemming from some old and obscure state law, Church-inspired but now Church-abandoned, that artificial insemination technically was adultery.

But what the hell was *double-diploidy?* Twice two was four, any fool knew that. Yet Dr. Fred must have had some reason for calling Sena a "double-diploid" instead of a tetraploid. And that reference to "schisming"—the awkward word was deliberate, an avoidance of "schizoid" or any other term that might have referred to Sena's psychology, and of "splitting" and similar terms which might have been geneticists' terminology; that sentence began with the crucial term "somatically"—body, not mind or germ cells.

Maurey was not a geneticist, but he knew his own background, and he was used to scientific shorthand. There was only one interpretation possible. Some of the twenty-four chromosome pairs which carried the human inheritance, and which should have been given to Sena in double measure, had not doubled. Had not *been* doubled, deliberately, for the placid failure of Dr. Fred's record to evince surprise betrayed foreplanning. Many of those that had doubled were still acting as sets-of-pairs rather than as groups-of-four—and of those, many had exhibited the peculiar gene-shuffling phenomenon called "crossing over," so that their genetic effects would not be traceable for generations except by the laborious process of chromosome mapping each generation—and even then only by someone who knew the fundamental secret Dr. Fred had written on this page.

Even more disturbing was that reference to "schisming" after RNA injections. It meant, surely, that Sena's inheritance had not been entirely fixed at birth, and that Dr. Fred had waited to fix it until Sena was physiologically mature; after that treatment, there had been some further change, undesirable but "slight," so that Dr. Fred thought it unnecessary to reshuffle Sena's genes with a DNA shot. She was "emergent stock"—a woman of no fortune, but with a name to come.

Maurey fingered the sore spot on his ear-lobe, the place from which Dr. Fred had taken the latest of his

periodic biopsies, as he took them from all his "children."
The spot stung to the salty perspiration on his fingertips,
and his whole body was shaking with fury and frustration.

The tetraploids were not the end of the story.

There was another form to come. Sena was the beginning of that line—and there was no telling where it might
lead, no telling how thoroughly the children of Dr. Fred's
tectogenesis might antiquate the giants. Sena looked like a
tetraploid—but her children would be—

What might Sena's children be, if she were allowed to
have them?

The puppy said "Urrgmph" and hit the floor on one
shoulder. She waddled over to Maurey and fell over on
her back, requiring that her tummy be scratched. Her
nearly hidden pink paps offered promises of thousands
and thousands of triploid puppies to follow her—

Or, perhaps, tetraploid puppies, with sex-linked double-
diploid characteristics hidden within them, to surprise
their antiquated tetraploid masters—or puppies ready to
change into crocodiles at a single DNA injection from Dr.
Fred, god, devil, all-father, master geneticist and tyrant
over all the polyploid world. . . .

With a growl Maurey snatched up the projector, which
had been resting on the bench beside the piles of paper.
The Brobdingnagian puppy, her chunky body all unknowingly the symbol of Maurey's and the giants' inevitable de-
feat, rolled over and crouched, laying back her ears.

The force-beam struck the stone floor at her side and
pitched her across the room. She got up, barking excitedly,
rump high, front paws spread. This time the reflected beam
caught her directly under the chin. She screamed and
brought up against the far wall.

Maurey laughed and turned the reflector to spread the
beam into a fan. The puppy regained her courage and
charged him, and Maurey broomed her back against the
wall again.

*Supersede the tetras, is it? We'll see which weapon can
be drawn the faster!*

He tumbled the dog this way and that, herded her into
the wastebasket, rolled the basket across the floor, overturned it, tumbled the yelping animal scrambling into a
corner and drove her out again—

"Maurice!"

Trembling, Maurey let go of the plunger. After a moment his eyes came into focus amid a haze of scalding tears.

It was Dr. Fred. Of course. No one else called him Maurice. The geneticist stood in the doorway. The dog whimpered and crawled toward him, her eyes darting back to Maurey in puzzlement.

"Maurice, what— I heard poor Decibelle a block away. What is that thing? Are you trying to kill her? And you've got my safe open! Have you lost your mind?"

Carefully, his fingernails digging into his palms, Maurey said:

"I wasn't hurting her, Dr. Fred. Admittedly she *sounds* like she's being murdered, she's so damned big." He realized suddenly that he was holding the silver muzzle of history's deadliest weapon directly in line with Dr. Fred's stomach, lowered it with enforced casualness, and laughed. That laugh came hard. "It was just a game—she was having as much fun as I was—"

Dr. Fred strode past him while he was still talking and bent over the stacked papers on the table.

"Why did you open my safe?"

Maurey gave him the prepared theorem. The exercise, since it had been mentally rehearsed, gave him time to calm down.

The rangy old man grumbled, almost like the puppy, while Maurey was talking.

"I can see *that*," he interrupted again. "But who gave you the combination?"

Nothing would be more suitable here than the truth, Maurey decided.

"You did."

"No, Maurice. My memory is not so bad as all that."

Maurey smiled. "But you did. You once opened the safe in my presence. I could hear the tumblers falling. It was musical; I remembered the tune. It was as simple as that."

"Really?" Dr. Fred said. "Now *there's* a phrase I loathe. Nothing is ever 'as simple as that.' "

" 'Nothing' is a very large term," Maurey said. "I've yet to encounter a sound too small for me to hear it, Dr. Fred. And my tonal memory is perfect."

"Well, I wish you'd told me that before," Dr. Fred

said, somewhat petulantly. "It'll have to be entered on your chart."

He riffled through the papers until he found Maurey's dossier, and pawed for the accompanying chromosome charts. The charts apparently were mislaid.

"Maurice, did you shuffle—? No no, they were in an awful hodge-podge before, I know. I really need a secretary, but they're all so bubble-headed. Come to see me— let me think—next Wednesday, will you, Maurice? I want to see if I can trace that auditory acuity. I *do* wish you'd told me before."

Exactly so. Dr. Fred was interested, and then had been diverted, by Maurey's sharpened talent. It had been chancey there for a moment, but in the long run it had proven far safer than telling Dr. Fred that some other person had given Maurey the combination to the safe. Dr. Fred might have checked that story; probably not, but he might have. He *would* check this one—and would find that it was true.

Maurey grinned another grin, secretly, all to himself. He had pushed the appropriate button, and the worn automaton before him had produced the predictable reaction. He had won again, as he would always win.

"I just noticed it myself a little while ago," he said. "Let's explore it by all means. Maybe there's more to it than, uh, meets the ear. I'd like to have a sonar sense, for instance."

"Now that's distinctly possible," Dr. Fred said. "Everyone does to a slight degree. An elegant notion, in fact. By all means."

"Next Wednesday," Maurey said, nodding. He went out.

He was still carrying the projector, dangling negligently from one hand at his side. Dr. Fred took no notice.

Maurey paused in the stairwell, considering how best to conceal it; he had of course left the newspapers on the floor of Dr. Fred's lab. Nothing occurred to him except to dismantle it, at least to the point where he had removed all the parts small enough to go in his pockets, and continue to carry the rest of it out in the open as though it were any ordinary chassis. He would have to chance meeting Sam, but the thing obviously had to go now to Maurey's own apartment, there was no other choice left.

His mind was now completely at ease. His body was still trembling a little, but that was an inevitable reaction, and it did not bother him.

Still, it would be a millenial day when the giants no longer needed to play-act with Dr. Fred—

And it would have to be soon.

V

The needle, hung by its point with a minute fleck of bees-wax, swung back and forth before the window with the regularity of a metronome. As it passed the central pane, Dr. Fred stabbed the waxed end of a thread into its eye and jerked it out again.

Back and forth. In and out.

After a while he was satisfied that his nerves were all right. He was mad clear through, and he was too old to risk such strong emotions. Every surge of adrenalin impaired his coordination, that coordination upon which microdissections and chromosome manipulation depended; every such surge raised his runaway blood pressure perilously near the blow-point of his sclerosing arteries, and destroyed forever a little more of his visual field. But he was all right, this time.

He bent again to examine Decibelle, who had laid her chin across his shoe-zipper. She seemed to be all right, too —except—Yes, she had cringed when he thumped her shoulder and told her she was a good girl. Now was she merely jumpy after the shocking mistreatment she had just suffered? Or was it—

A sudden yelp left his question open for the moment. He squatted all the way down and ran his fingers gently over her bone structure until he was satisfied that she had at least two cracked ribs. She also cowered at every sudden move. Maurice's "toy," whatever it had been, *had* injured her, and it had scared her almost out of her considerable wits.

Dr. Fred wondered what it was. Something electronic, by the look of it. In the old days, sadistic kids had shot household amonia solutions into dogs' eyes with water pistols. Nowadays they hitched the poor beasts to spark coils or something even more elaborate, but in the end it was just

57

the ancient tin-can torture. It didn't even make any difference whether the kids were tetraploid or just ordinary
diploid kids; they satisfied their power-fantasies with equivalent cruelties.

He stood up to dial the number of the veterinarian who
had administered all of Decibelle's preventive shots, and
considered the matter further. It did make a difference, of
course. The giants, even the best of them, had to live in a
world which was actively and pointedly hostile. The diploids, except for some few—if much publicized—minor-
ities, had only the general wastefulness of nature against
them. Earthquakes hate nobody; but the diploids—

The diploids hated the giants, as well as each other, and
had the means to implement it. The psychology of that
hatred was obscure. Field tests had tended to show that
what one might assume to be the most obvious sources of
diploid jealousy—the longevity and the almost incredible
physical toughness of the giants—actually aroused only the
most remote, the most intellectualized dislikes. The tha-
lamic disturbance, the hatred that really chewed into the
guts, was directed toward the tetras' size first of all, and
then toward the makeshift social systems their near-sterility
and lack of living quarters other than the university dorms
had forced them to contrive. Subconsciously, perhaps, the
average diploid wanted to be a giant, and felt himself frus-
trated; yet—let his children be tetras? Never; no advantage could compensate for the stigma of being so different.
Well—hardly ever.

And there were stories of another sort, springing up out
of the oppressive sense of sexual inadequacy the giant wom-
en aroused, and aided in their circulation by the known
limited fertility of the tetraploid organism. *You know what
they say about their women? Freemartins, that's what. A
fellow I know told me . . .* one of a thousand scabrous jokes.
And there were stories—most of them, unfortunately, true
—about Polly Follmer; the prettiest (as well as the dumb-
est) tetra who ever disappeared up the pike. She had
wound up, after a brief but spectacular spell as Miss Cow
Country, in a thoroughly rumor-encrusted obscurity. The
little fellow with the height fetish, Tommy Boyston, who
still had vaults full of money left after buying—and buying off—six long-legged specimens of living calendar art,
one after the other, after commissioning the two larger-

than-life and realistically tinted statues entitled "Prone" and "Supine" that still indicated the lay of the land on his estate; and after throwing a three-day Sweet Sixteen party for Polly that was still the talk of the international set, had married her. He had, indeed, bought pretty Polly and put her in a gilded pumpkin shell, where—still delighted with his bargain—he kept her in the most stupefying luxury. Very well. Polly had found what she wanted, perhaps even what she deserved—she was incredibly beautiful, the only redhead of her kind—and Dr. Fred did not begrudge it her, although she might well have done tetra women as a group incalculable harm. Then, too, there was a predatory type of diploid woman—not always by any means unmarried—for whom the tetraploid men were natural prey. There were jokes about that, too.

The emotional disturbances among the giants were becoming more and more pronounced as the pressures increased. This tormenting of a harmless puppy was the most upsetting incident yet. It had done more than shock him. It had shaken the very basis of his plans for the giants, as a temblor worries the foundations of an old and settled house.

Well, as soon as the vet came and strapped up those ribs, he would take Decibelle up to his cabin and nurse her back to a semblance of love and trust. Actually, he would be able to spend only the evenings there; his academic day was scheduled to the bursting point, always. Who, then? Sena, of course. She was a prime favorite with Decibelle, and he had no doubt she would spell him daytimes. Since she had never been known to cut class for frivolous reasons, she no doubt had all her cuts coming. So that settled that; and yet—the problem remained.

The swinging needle slowed gradually, its path turning with the Earth's rotation while Dr. Fred pondered; at last it hit the window glass and twisted to a stop. The tinny impact reminded him of why he had put it up there. That shock, that moment when he had seen Maurice's beautifully balanced mind wobbling toward paranoia, had frightened him more than he liked to admit. It had been reassuring to find that it had not troubled the neuromuscular coördination which was his stock in trade.

But the essential, the ideational shock remained. If the best intelligence among the giants was inclining already toward the easy excuse of persecution, if it had already tipped far enough to fall into the compensation of sadism, then the plan for the tetras which Dr. Fred had evolved was too long-term to work.

It was that realization which had reduced him to talking like a senile old man, like a soap-opera doctor, before Maurice, in order to conceal his fear. It had been pure foolishness to pretend that Maurice had critically disturbed the order of the papers. Nothing went into the safe which had not been culled too thoroughly to require the dim-brained expedients of mechanical filing. He hoped that the giant hadn't noticed the slip; he'd seemed mighty upset himself—a mildly hopeful sign up to a point. Of course a sense of guilt has a threshold; at a certain level of intensity it begins to reinforce the habit-pattern rather than inhibit it—

But Maurice had been sorting the papers, too. And Maurice, though he were as mad as the Hatter, was the most alert of all the tetras. He might have seen Sena's papers, and understood them.

He would have understood them had he seen them. And he would have understood, then, some of the ingredients of the time-bomb Dr. Fred had planted beneath giants and diploids alike.

Maurice would not be able, now, to await the explosion. He would be perfectly ready to kill Dr. Fred to snuff it out—

Except that killing Dr. Fred would not snuff it out. There was only one death which could defuse that bomb. Dr. Fred spread the documents out over the table with a broad sweep of both hands. The code symbols relating to Sena leaped out to his eyes. He snatched the fascicles out of the fan and riffled through them. Chromatin records—molecular film analyses—histology lab reports—genealogical summary—

The somatic record was gone.

Whatever might come of actual genetic mutations, the type theorists called cataclysmic, there was implicit in Sena the final flowering of the possibilities of *Homo sapiens*—whereas a mutated man would be in actuality a new species, not *H. sapiens* at all. Those possibilities were all implicit in her somatic record, the first full-length portrait of humanity-to-come. And report and possibilities alike were in the hands of Goliath of the Philistines—a giant, and—

A madman.

Dr. Fred considered the tears flowing along the creases besides his nose with bitterly academic interest.

Methfessel closed the locker room door, shot the bolt, and pointed across the low-ceiling room. The gesture was unnecessary; the golden battle uniforms compelled attention in the drab cement enclosure like a fanfare of clarions. There was one suit hanging in each dull green locker, tenantless, yet perfect and beautiful with a life of its own.

Maurey strode to the nearest one and examined it with admiration.

"First class workmanship," he said at once. "Did you use the list of contractors I sent you? Everything fits so perfectly into everything else, you'd think it'd all been done by the same company."

"I used the list, and told 'em all to be strict as hell about the tolerances," Methfessel said. "And it cost maybe five times as much as it should have, doing it that way."

"It would have cost you your whole investment if any one outfit had figured out what the end-product was going to be," Maurey retorted. "If you're going to use your head for nothing but counting your money, Ira, you can at least tackle the job realistically."

Methfessel shrugged, and Maurey resumed examining the uniform. The basic part of the armor was a heavy breastplate, hinged to close over chest and back like the carapace and plastron of a turtle. At the bottom of the plate was a brief metal skirt of overlapping leaves, serving as both guard and belt; a control box, mounting a single large red master button and four smaller black ones, was placed to hang over the left hip of the wearer, and on the right was a holster of plastic straps. The gun in that holster was in some respects like the first projector of the one-way-push—but compressed, trimmed, balanced into a proper side-arm.

"No cold flask?" Maurey said, hefting the gun. "I see there's an input lead to the control box there; that'll make it a bit awkward to manipulate."

"You couldn't prove it by me," Methfessel said, shrugging again. "I sent your figures and the prints to your captive genius, what's-his-name, Kelland, and he designed this stuff. I wouldn't know a cold flask from a hot rock."

Maurey grunted and put the pistol back into the webbing. He was none too sure that he approved of the whole idea of a force-pistol, anyhow; it seemed a trifle overt. Maybe a lance would have been better after all. But the thing was done.

Anyhow, the real wonder of the armor was the thing that hung poised on the back plate, like an eagle spread to abduct a lamb. In some respects it resembled a comic-strip "flying belt"—which it was—but it was elaborately feathered with delicate flanges, titled to apply the one-way push over the greatest possible area without at the same time materially increasing the air-resistance, and so seemed to have more "futuristic" superfluous ornament than anything ever drawn by Dick Calkins.

Maurey was confident that the device did not have a non-functioning square inch, whatever its appearance. Every other flange broadcast the reactionless energy; the alternate flanges picked it up and turned it into mechanical motion. Warping fields, designed to waste controlled portions of the energy as the dove wings of the ancient *Taube* monoplane had wasted flying speed, did away with any need for direct methods of steering; they were actuated by movements of the wearer's body. The device had no moving parts; but it would steer with great delicacy.

Finally, there was a helmet, or more exactly, a casque. It was linked electrically with the flight mechanism and with the force pistol. Maurey could not decide at once what it was for; his sketch had called for a fishbowl. This was topped by a short spike, flanged as if to bleed off heat or some other kind of waste radiation, but that seemed to be purely decorative. It was a true Buck Rogers touch, jarringly out of key with the known superbly functional design of the rest.

"What's that?" Maurey said, pointing.

"For protection," Ira said. "I don't know why. Maybe you're supposed to ram the opposition. I don't know anything about this kind of thing, Maurey."

"Kelland didn't say how it 'protected'?"

"Not to me. It's called a 'transcaster' on the prints."

There seemed to be no present answer to that puzzle. It would take a thorough examination of the circuits to understand why Kelland had put that little Christmas tree on top of the casque. Maurey suspected that the reason would turn out to be as exciting as the rest of the apparatus. The armor was a work of genius; it was a good thing, considering the amount of understanding of Maurey's aims that it evinced, that Kelland was a giant, and from Maurey's special point of view a dumb giant at that.

They were all dumb giants when it came to military theory, for that matter. As undergraduates they should have been required to take a minimum of two years of ROTC, since Dunhill was a land-grant college; but the Army too had rules, and the current pertinent one here was that no soldier may be taller than six feet four. Maurey had subsequently stolen a full set of ROTC textbooks and maintained them in his own locker until he had milked them dry. They were years behind the times even in terms of diploid warfare, and for the kind of warfare Maurey had in mind they would have been worse than useless, anyhow. For that he would make up his own tactics, as soon as he had finished perfecting his strategy. He enjoyed thinking about how surprised the career officers who taught Dunhill's ROTC courses would be when he fired *his* opening gun.

"What gets me," Ira said in an aggrieved tone, "is that the guy didn't allow for any protection for the arms or legs. I'd have thought he'd design a complete body-armor while he was at it—like our football uniforms."

"He must have had a reason," Maurey said abstractedly. "By the way, speaking of football, did Sam Ettinger come to see you yet?"

"That's the bird that walked off the field when Hammy was hurt. Yeah. I took him back in, like you said. But I don't mind telling you I don't trust him. He's a malcontent."

Maurey smiled crookedly.

"I don't know any well-adjusted tetras, Ira," he said.

"That's not what I mean. He's what we used to call 'disaffected' in the last Last War. Too full of ideas of his own to follow orders. Oh, well, you're calling it."

"Either way, you make money," Maurey pointed out. "Which reminds me: make me out a check for twenty-five thousand."

"What the hell for?"

"I want you to buy the dormitory grounds where we're living, and that's the price the University set."

"Think again," Methfessel said flatly. "What do I want with those firetraps? I'll need all the cash I've got to enlarge the stadium. Paying for that armor was no pink tea, Maurey."

"You'll make the money back at the first tournament," Maurey declared. "And as long as the University is housing the giants, it's got entirely too much say over what they do. Don't you realize that it'll be sure to prohibit the tournaments as soon as the word leaks through? *Then* you'd be in a nice mess."

"What's to prevent them from threatening to fire everybody concerned, anyhow?"

"Don't be silly. By this time, Dunhill University *is* the tetras, as far as the public is concerned. Do you think they'd throw away their best drawing card? And lose twenty-five per cent of their faculty at the same time?"

Methfessel thought about it. It was obvious that he was aware that Maurey had additional reasons for the proposal, without knowing what they were; but where money was involved, he was unlikely to ask for a second reason unless the first one seemed insufficient.

"I've got to act as if you knew what you're doing," he said finally. He pulled out his checkbook. "Here. Just be sure you spend it all in the same place."

VI

Dr. Fred blew his cork.

"I don't understand you any more, Maurice," he stormed, pacing back and forth before his laboratory bench. "This is far and away the most high-handed thing I ever heard of. The University's relations with that promoter already are quite dubious enough—this modern system of semi-professional handling of college sports is vicious, in my opinion. I should have supposed a research project like ours, at least, to have been immune to such exploitation, yet here you are actually encouraging it—and what's more, turning us all over to a commercial scheme like so many sacks of potatoes!"

"Nothing of the sort, Dr. Fred," Maurey said patiently. "I didn't make the offer, and I didn't accept it. The only choice I had was to refuse to act as the go-between, in which case somebody else would have been found. I agree with you that the gap between the University and Ira Methfessel isn't wide enough by several miles, but I chose simply to be realistic about it.

"As for the tournaments, I take exactly the opposite view (nor were they my idea either, by the way). They give us an opportunity to make a living, and quite a good one, without being dependent upon University charity, and that's something we've all needed a long time for the sake of our self-respect. Granted that it's not a very dignified living, but we're in no position to be so choosey."

Dr. Fred stopped his pacing and looked steadily at the lounging giant over the tops of his glasses.

"You haven't said anything yet that I don't think a half-truth or a plain fantasy," he said. "I'll pass your curious conception of 'realistic' behavior; that kind of expediency is no novelty to the world, heaven knows. For the rest—well, evidently you think that by making the tetraploid

project over into a business venture, you weaken Methfessel's direct hold on University affairs. Do I have that
right? Then that's a half-truth. The other side of the coin
is that at the same time you've ruined the University's reputation more thoroughly than could any possible relationship with professional sports. Twenty-five thousand dollars!
What can the Board have been thinking of? They might
just as well have sold the whole chemistry department,
students included, to Columbia Pharmaceuticals across the
river!"

His eyes darkened. "Come to think of it, we're lucky
they didn't. You were just a boy when the great urine-jug
hassel broke out. The Board let Columbian sell them on
putting a fifty-gallon jug with a funnel in it into every
urinal on campus—for hormone research, they said, but of
course Columbian sold every microgram of testosterone
they got out of those jugs at a fearsome profit, and all the
students got out of it was weeks of bad smells—

"No, don't interrupt, please, Maurice. That's only the
beginning; I apologize for my digression. I suppose you
realize also that this affair terminates the polyploidy research as far as I can be concerned. Now that the giants
are living on privately-owned property, they will have to be
treated like any other faculty member, graduate assistant or
scholarship student. The social aspects of the study go out
the window, nor will I have any authority to direct or in
any other way interfere with the genetic course of the experiment. I'm left with nothing but a group of volunteers."

Dr. Fred snorted.

"Volunteers!" he said. "No wonder the so-called 'social
sciences' were a bust! 'Will one or two atoms of oxygen
kindly step forward and answer a few carefully impersonal
questions?' "

Maurey started to speak, then halted before his lips had
parted. Better to let the old man talk it all out.

"What the reaction of the public will be to this I don't
know exactly," Dr. Fred went on, a little more quietly,
"but it's bound to be bad. I can only hope that it won't
be extreme. You've expelled your brothers into the status
private citizen, and you're going to find that that's a much
more dangerous and humiliating status than the one you
had before, the one the public equated with that of ex-
perimental animals. No, your motives may be spotless,

Maurice—though I shan't say I believe that—but good or bad your *actions* have been despicable."

Dr. Fred turned his back on Maurey abruptly and stared out the smudged window. Maurey waited a moment more, but nothing else was forthcoming now. Very well, then:

"I rather expected some such reaction," Maurey said evenly, "but I certainly didn't anticipate so much violence. It's unlike you to use such loaded terms, Dr. Fred. The mere fact of a change of ownership in some property is not going to change your relationship to us in the least. The tetras all owe their existence, let alone their biological advantages, to you, and they won't forget it. They'll still be exactly where they were before, physically; the fact that that bit of land can't be called 'campus' any more changes nothing on the event-level, it only changes a word.

"They'll still come to you and coöperate with you in your experiments. They'll look to you for guidance as before. They love you; you know that. Your anathemas on 'volunteers' do nothing but obscure the fact that we were always volunteers. You never did have any dictatorship over our personal lives, nor did you ever try to exercise any—*not until now*—so it seems foolish in you to complain that any real control has been taken away from you. What you had before, you have now."

"Yes, yes, Maurice," Dr. Fred said wearily. He did not turn. "I am not as unaware of the difference between real meaning and formal meaning as you'd have me think. I heard you shift, for instance, from '*they* love you' to '*we* were always volunteers'; perhaps you didn't even hear yourself do that, but to an outsider it would have been very marked. And your speech tells me what you see: a feeble old man, querulous over the intervention of cold reality between himself and his pet hobby. I withdraw my implied accusation of bad faith, which I had no right to state. But I believe you are as aware as I am that what you have done will have evil consequences for the giants—not for me, Maurice, but for the giants. Incidentally, what did you want Sena's somatic record for?"

"I didn't want it," Maurey said, freezing inside. "Am I supposed to have it? And what has it to do with what we're talking about, anyhow?"

"I would very much like to know," Dr. Fred said.

"However your course plainly does not include me, so I shan't pursue the matter. When you're through with it, let me know."

"I don't have it."

"All right. You may as well go, Maurice. You can't undo what you've done in any case, nor can I expect to talk you out of whatever it is you're planning. But I will tell you this: your sanity is dubious."

"I'll go," Maurey said. "Since we've reached the wild accusation stage already, the matter is closed. Goodbye, Dr. Fred."

"Goodbye, Maurice."

Maurey closed the door with precision and went down the squeaky old wooden stairs, stairs worn shiny and canted alarmingly around their central obelisk of stale air by generations of students. Biology Hall had burned down after it was a century old, but had been rebuilt to the same specs, and now even the restoration was ready to go up as soon as some fated cigarette butt brought it to the flash point.

On the whole, though he was a little angry—that couldn't be helped, and consequently there was no point in resenting it—he was well satisfied with the way the interview had gone. Most of the giants, he was sure, would be glad to be out from under the fatherly eye of the University, or would decide that they were pleased after they had gotten used to the idea. They would come to Dr. Fred, of course, but they would find the old man accusing Maurey of some heinous plot the details of which he would not be able to give.

The end-product would be a strengthening of his own already considerable influence (since, although he would deny engineering the transfer of the property, the impression of himself as prime mover would remain after the denial) and an abrupt slump in Dr. Fred's prestige. Of course, Dr. Fred might not react as predicted, but in view of his just-concluded performance that danger was small, and in a few days it would no longer matter what he said or did.

He stood for a moment on the stone porch of the building, looking over the campus. It was late in the afternoon; probably Sena and Sam would eat at the student cafeteria, which Maurey loathed—if he never saw another boiled Brussels sprout in his life it would be too soon. For a moment he was prompted to let the matter wait until tomorrow, but then thought better of it. Providing properly for the future entailed so many unpleasant tasks that were each one postponed only a single day, the future would never arrive at all.

He got the roader out and drove it over to Sena's dorm, where he left a note for her. Then he proceeded to the men's dormitory, where he let himself into Sam's room with a passkey. Sam's typewriter had a half-finished letter in it, but its content was uninteresting. Maurey selected Martin Johnson's *Art and Scientific Thought* from Sam's bookshelves and made himself comfortable.

Sena arrived first. She was somewhat flushed, but her heightened color in no way diminished the effect of her honey-colored hair and the pale blue *tailleur*.

"I got a terrible ragging from some of the kids on the first floor," she said. "Are you sure it's all right for me to be here, Maurey?"

He looked at her appreciatively. He could never decide whether she made all her own clothes, like some of the tetras, or patronized the Domestic Arts majors (diploid) who needed extra cash. Whichever, on her it was stunning.

"Quite sure, my dear. I'll explain as soon as Sam arrives. I must warn you that the situation's rather complex —and not without its unpleasant aspects."

"Really? How ominous!" Sena sat down neatly on the edge of Sam's cot, raising her eyebrows in mild alarm. "Can't you—oh, that sounds like Sam now."

Maurey's supernormal hearing had already detected Sam humming under his breath at the foot of the stairwell; as an undergraduate, he had played in the student orchestra, and when he was most content he could usually be heard humming the third trombone part of The Star Spangled Banner, apparently without being aware of it. Since the part consisted mostly of a single repeated note, it made Sam sound rather like Morse code recorded at 78 rpm and played back at 16.

When he entered, the black-haired giant's surprise was comical.

"What are you trying to do, you two, get me thrown

out?" he demanded, half seriously. "After I went back to Maurey's crazy football team? There's gratitude for you!"

Maurey grinned and explained what had happened to the dormitory title.

"So this is a private apartment now, Sam, and you can have a woman in it if you like."

"I like," Sam said immediately, Sena smiled.

"I thought you would. But there's a hitch. I knew that as soon as you heard the news, you and Sena would want to follow through on your commitment—your housing problem is already practically a legend on campus, you know. So I wanted to talk to you both right away, and try and persuade you not to do it."

"*Not* to do it?" they said together. Sena leaned forward. "What do you mean, Maurey?" she said.

"Sena, how much do you know about yourself—about your genetic makeup, that is?"

"Why, not a great deal," she admitted, frowning slightly. "About what we all know about ourselves. I know who my parents were, and that one of them was related to Dr. Fred. And I know the theory of chromosome-doubling, of course."

"That's what I thought. Do you know any more than that, Sam?"

"About myself?"

"No," Maurey said. "About Sena."

Sam shook his head, patently mystified. Maurey paused a moment. He realized that he liked Sam, and he wondered if it were really necessary to be so brutal. The two kids loved each other; wouldn't it be enough to persuade them not to have a child?

He realized at once that the suggestion would be just as badly received as his earlier one had been. The low fertility of the giants had made birth control close to a crime among them; and besides, what if there should be an accident? A tremor of pure terror made him catch his breath.

"I hate to say this, but it's got to be said," he declared. "Sena, I've seen your records; Dr. Fred showed them to me. And you're *not a tetraploid*."

Sena went white, and one hand flew to her throat.

"I'm—not?" she said faintly.

"I'm afraid not. Essentially—forgive me, both of you, but

this thing transcends all of us—essentially you're diploid. Your size is tectogenetic in origin, you were given that one characteristic by direct manipulation—one of Dr. Fred's famous micro-operations on the genes. It was fixed as a transform with an RNA injection; you probably remember that, Sena."

"DNA," Sena said. "I remember, but it was DNA, and it was long after I was grown to full size."

"No, it was RNA—not to alter the genes, but to fix the effect in the cytoplasm. Dr. Fred didn't tell you that, but that was what it was. So if you and Sam have a child, it won't be tetraploid. It will be triploid. Like Decibelle."

"Are you sure, Maurey?" Sam said slowly. "Why would Dr. Fred pull a trick like that? He told me that the dog was strictly an experiment, and that he hadn't gotten around for testing triploidy in humans."

"And so he hasn't, of course; Dr. Fred wouldn't tell you anything that wasn't so! But when Sena's child is born, there's his test. As for why—Well, naturally, scientific curiosity must have been one reason. He had to provide a diploid human being to mate with a tetraploid, so naturally he had to supply one of practicable size."

There was a brief silence. At last Sam said:

"Maurey, I'm sorry, but I can't swallow that. Dr. Fred's not underhanded. He would have told Sena, and when he knew who Sena was going to live with, he would have told him, too. In this case, me."

"That's right," Sena agreed. "You must have misunderstood him, Maurey. After all, you're not a geneticist, even though you are our biggest brain."

Maurey shook his head.

"There was no reason for him to tell anybody. You've seen for yourself what a Blue Ox that dog is; would you have known it for a triploid if Dr. Fred hadn't told you? Of course you wouldn't. And your child would look like a tetra, too, just as Sena looks like one."

"But the reason, Maurey, the reason!" Sam said.

"I can't be sure," Maurey said. "But Dr. Fred's an old man, and he doesn't think as straight as he used to. When I objected to this whole business, he turned on me in a white rage—I was flabbergasted, let me tell you. The first thing I wanted to know was why he couldn't have implanted tetraploid male germ cells in a diploid woman, artificially, instead of creating all this incipient heartbreak. That was when he lost him temper, so I never did get any answer.

"However, it's my guess that he doesn't think the tetras to have been a successful experiment, and so he's planting ringers among us. Sena is almost surely not the only one. In a few generations we'll be cut back down to diploid size again—we'll *be* diploids—without ever knowing exactly how or why it happened. And nobody will try the experiment again—because by that time the existing laws against chromosome-doubling in human beings will be given a full set of teeth. Hell, I'm not even sure *I'm* not a phony—you can imagine what a shock this was to me. I think I can claim to know just how you both feel. But, there it is."

Sam swore and sat down abruptly, feeling for the arm of his chair with the gesture of a man gone suddenly weak in the knees. Sena was blinking, unsuccessfully trying to squeeze back tears. Maurey felt simultaneously like a louse and like a composer whose sonata has just been afforded on ovation.

"Of course it's hard to take, damned hard," he said. "I don't ask you to bolt it down whole, or expect you to. As Sena says, I might have misinterpreted what I saw. That might just possibly account for Dr. Fred's being so angry with me. I'd be delighted to be proven wrong, believe me. One of you ought to check me."

"I'll talk to him," Sam said. "I can't quite see you telling us this if it isn't so, Maurey, but of course we'll have to be sure you haven't gone off half-cocked." His voice wavered dubiously as he reached the end of the sentence. "Damnation! We'll really be out in the cold if it's true."

"Life is aye full of cark and cauld," Sena said. The attempt to be cheerful was pitifully futile. "I won't get *any* man, big or little, if I am just a phony. But Maurey, I'm nearly thirty years old, and I was just getting out of an awful ten-year adolescence when I was twenty-two. Doesn't that disprove your theory?"

"I wish it did," Maurey said somberly. "But unfortunately it doesn't prove anything either way. You'd have to be long-lived in order to seem like a tetra, so Dr. Fred might have given you that characteristic too, for the purposes of the masquerade. Or, you might be a true tetra, and I've caused all this fuss for nothing. I can only say that I wouldn't have opened my mouth if I hadn't been close to positive about it. All I want to know now is this: Do you agree with me that, if it *is* true, Sena should not—should not bear any children?"

"No," Sam said. His voice was gravelly. "For all we know, Dr. Fred might be right. The tetras might have turned out to be an unsuccessful experiment. I'm convinced that you mean well, Maurey—hell, I've never known you to be wrong on anything this important. But I won't commit us to anything until I've checked."

"Fair enough," Maurey agreed, rising. He was glad that Sam had chosen to be stubborn; it banished the last traces of that momentary regret he had felt at the beginning of the gambit. Sam was thoroughly likeable, but in this chess-game no piece was indispensable.

"Check," Maurey said.

VII

By the next day, the story somehow had become common stock among the giants, though Sam was reluctant to believe that Maurey had been circulating it in advance of conclusive evidence. Possibly some part, if not all, of the discussion in Sam's dorm room had been overheard—voices had a way of leaking out under doors, and the cement stairwell made a passable whispering gallery; nor could any tetra be condemned for eavesdropping upon a matter of such intimate and personal importance to all of them.

At first the reactions varied widely. There was flat incredulity—

"Sam, who's mad at Sena? Somebody's spreading the gawdamndest fairy tale!"

and reluctant sympathy—

"Tough luck, Sam. It must be pretty rough on you, too."

as well as immediate tetraploid chauvinism—

"Good thing you found out in time, eh, old man?"

There was also a startling amount of covert hostility. Some of the giants went out of their way to avoid the embarrassment, or the humiliation, of speaking to Sam.

It was still worse to find that a few of the giants had not shucked off the predatory vices of the diploids with their size. Several of them, Sena reported, seemed to have concluded that Sena needed "consolation" and would therefore be easy pickings. This shameful reminder of a common, ignoble ancestry troubled Sam most, although he could not say quite why he found it so ominous.

And nothing could be done about it. Dr. Fred was out of town, attending a world congress of geneticists in Toronto. As the month went by, Sena's presumptive diploidy receded gradually as *the* subject of conversation among the giants, and was replaced by a gathering excitement over the new private-citizen status and the Paying Job. There was also a good deal of speculation over a possible revival of the tournament idea, though neither Methfessel nor Maurey had mentioned it in over a month.

Underneath all this Sam saw the reactions to his and Sena's problem begin to divide and flow away from one another in two definite streams. The unbelievers and the sympathizers showed a tendency to merge into a common camp of sympathy for the outcasts; while the chauvinists, the suspicious, and the rejected wolves clumped together elsewhere, more slowly, like blood-cells in an antagonistic serum.

Even grimmer portents were visble to Sam, whose deep personal involvement had sensitized him to the slightest signs of new trends. The division among the giants began to express itself in terms of the two teams on which they were now earning their living.

Tetras sympathetic to Sam and Sena, naturally enough, predominated in the Titans, where Sam played. As a result, the members of the minority faction began drifting over to the Atlanteans—where the same phenomenon was taking place in reverse. Methfessel, who now managed both teams, did not attempt to block the exchanges; indeed, Sam suspected him of encouraging it.

Certainly it was to Methfessel's advantage, for it brought the rivalry between the two teams—heretofore only a desultory, token rivalry at best—to a state of real acrimony, and the games became rough almost to the point of viciousness. The crowds loved it. The games always had partaken of the spirit of a mass gladiatorial contest—a spirit which is entirely a function of the temper of the spectators, not of what specific game is being played on the field—and now the players were accommodating themselves to that mood. The gate increased at once; the stands were packed for almost every game.

And the percentage of on-the-field injuries increased enormously.

Before Dr. Fred came back, it was already too late to scotch the schisming of these two camps even with any statement that there was nothing to Maurey's soft denunciation. Something had happened—Sam could not find out what—which had blighted Dr. Fred's authority among the tetras. They spoke of him in a way they had never spoken before, in a tone which regardless of the words had contempt beneath it. After all, the tone said, he's a diploid—he created us, but all the same, he's a diploid.

Sam tried all day to reach him upon his return, but Sam's own rigid schedule was in the way. He reached the geneticist at last, by phone, at four in the afternoon just before a field trip with a Skyhook cosmic-ray balloon, and then the old man evaded Sam's necessarily cautious questions and asked to see him at once, which was of course impossible. Sam had to settle for an appointment at 6:00 A.M. of the next day.

He thought at once of spending part of the evening with Sena, or better yet, all of it; but urgent though the impulse was, sober consideration told him that it would be the worst move he could make. It had not always been so, but now they were no longer new young lovers for whom a tumble into bed assuaged all griefs and swept all problems away, at least until the knock of dawn on the windowpane.

It was sad to have lost that (though Sam sometimes suspected that he regretted its passing slightly more than Sena did); but what they had gained from it—which was also its price—was the knowledge that love is not only an intoxicant, but an inexorable code of laws firmly derived from antecedents in the future. To drown one's sorrows in it is as surely fatal as jumping off a high building for the fun of being in free fall.

If Sam and Sena had not known that before, certainly Maurey's gambit with their future children—it was not even his own pieces he was proposing to sacrifice!—would have made it more than clear enough. Knowing that, it would be impossible for them to resort now to love-making as though it were no more than a deliberately unwise Martini. And their situation was already dismal enough, without their sitting for three or four hours staring miserably at each other, trying to find something to say, or proffering each other comfort where there was as yet no rational reassurance to be had.

He called her, and told her of the appointment with Dr. Fred. Her quiet understanding made him feel a little better, but a moment later he was doubly aware of how desperate he had become. He was already grasping at the smallest straw.

Being alone in his room was even worse, however. He could not concentrate on his technical books for more than three minutes without becoming conscious all over again of the all-gone feeling in the pit of his stomach, and the troubles of fictional characters filled him with a furious impatience; Emma Bovary had enthralled him for years, but now she seemed liked a fool who had invented troubles in the absence of any real ones.

At midnight he had enough, and threw himself out of his room without stopping to lock the door or put out the goose-neck desk lamp. He felt as though he had nothing left which it would be worth anyone's bother to steal.

The long, aimless walk through the dim campus brought him finally to the edge of the river. He sat down amid the sedges on the steep-sloping bank and began to chuck stones into the black water. Each stone distorted the reflections of the lights of Columbian Pharmaceuticals on the other side, turning them into cold, wiggling flames. The wind was away from him tonight, blowing toward the factory, for which he was grateful; at least he would not have to breathe the notorious "Columbian Pew," which on some days made the whole campus smell of adhesive tape.

After a great while he stopped throwing rocks and just sat, hugging his knees. The circling of his own thoughts numbed him, and the images on the water writhed hypnotically even without the help of Sam's stones. . . .

Across the water there was a shrill, mournful hooting. He blinked and sat himself up straight, feeling cramped and emotionally washed out. The river was heavily enshrouded in a rising mist. The hoot, he realized slowly, was the plant whistle, calling in the third of the firm's staggered shifts—the lobster trick. That made it 4:00 A.M. His watch confirmed it.

Might as well walk slowly over to Biology Hall and wait for Dr. Fred to arrive. The wait would be tedious now that he was more awake, but some time could be killed by cutting through town and picking up breakfast at an all-night beanery. Curiously, he was ravenously hungry; he had thought he would be too upset to eat, but evidently his body was paying very little attention to his mind. He climbed the sandy bank and began to walk, favoring his stiff muscles.

He had a hot dog with "the works" at the Greek's, taking his time, but still the clock advanced hardly at all. It was just dawn by the time he came in sight of Biology Hall. No one was stirring. It seemed a shame that such a peace should ever be broken, spurious though it was. He went up the broad river of steps, paused, and went inside, where it was warmer; he was, he realized suddenly, chilled through.

The door of Dr. Fred's laboratory was ajar. Before Sam touched it he could see that the safe was standing open. Papers were tumbled out of it in a frozen cascade. His stomach muscles knotted.

A robbery? But why would anybody want to steal anything from Dr. Fred? His work had no military significance, and was of no monetary value—

He felt the answer searing its way up toward the surface of his mind. Anything was better than having to face it. He lunged through the door.

His first impulse after that was to run headlong back the way he had come and throw himself into the dawn-bloody river.

Dr. Fred would not have to wait for the massive stroke, or the series of little ones, with which his high blood pressure would have ended his life later this year. He was tumbled grotesquely on the boards, half under the workbench. His cheek and shoulder rested in a sticky black pool. In spite of his twisted position, it was easy to see that his entire rib-cage had been smashed in by some single, unimaginable blow.

Decibelle growled, barring all her teeth. Then, recognizing Sam, she lifted her chin from the dead man's shoe. Whining urgently, she began to crawl toward him on her belly. Sam bent abstractedly and put out a trembling hand toward the dog, but his eyes had already found the weapon and could not leave it.

It lay shattered in the farthest corner of the room, the one that was always darkest during the work-day. Now it was directly in the merciless early sunlight; and, despite its almost total breakage, he recognized it.

He had made it.

It was the projector of the one-way push.

BOOK TWO

VIII

All but a small percentage of Americans live out their lives without ever coming closer to murder than the daily tabloid can bring them, though magazine fiction (nobody reads books) and television confer a spurious intimacy with the subject. Sam was no exception. To say that he was overwhelmed with horror and fear is to say nothing, for, although true, the phrases did not correspond with the feeling: the emotions he suffered were horror and fear, but they were entirely unlike any emotions he had ever before associated with those words.

He realized that he should be doing something, but nothing occurred to him that was not wildly irrelevant. He simply squatted, absurdly scratching the half-grown dog and trying to think—not a rational thought, but just any thought at all. His whole mind was fragmented. Perhaps the most terrifying thing still was that instant searing flash he had felt at the moment he had first seen the body, that stab of *guilt*. Traces of it still remained, unexpungeable by mere certainty that he was innocent.

Partly, of course, the guilty feeling had come from an underlying consciousness of being in a bad position. Dr. Fred had been murdered while Sam was sitting by the river, alone, unable to account for his time. He had left his room light on, which would look like an amateur's attempt to establish an alibi. And a motive could be shown, a motive stronger than many a one which had hung accused men before. It was all there.

But the sensation had been stronger than simple fear. It had had all the flavor of conviction, of a compulsive self-knowledge: *"I did it."* It had brought out the buried guilt of the out-group, of the man on the defensive, the man whose real guilt—so easily confused with other, lesser guilts—is that of being different from his fellows.

All these fragments fluttered confusedly inside his skull for well over two seconds. His first formulated thought was: Would a statistical study of the neurotics who run to the police with "confessions" of every publicized crime show a predominance of minority-group members?

The question was so outrageously remote from any "proper" reaction to murder—as such reactions were taught in the video school—that he could scarcely smother a hysterical giggle. But it freed him. He found that he could think again, with at least passable coherence. He gave the huge puppy a final pat and stood up.

It would be at best futile, at worst damning, to sneak out and let someone else discover the pitiful corpse. He was fairly saddled with it, and the real killer had planned nothing else. This much had to be accepted at the beginning. Sam knew that he could not hope to out-plan such a man from a standing start. He would have to consolidate his own position within the frame of a probable death-cell.

He had one advantage. The killer could not have anticipated that Sam would find the murder out at dawn, unless he had tapped Dr. Fred's telephone and had so learned of the early-morning appointment. That would require a vigilance at monitoring Dr. Fred's calls which Sam was convinced was impossible for anyone whose funds were limited, and who needed to pretend to a normal schedule at the same time.

Probably it had not even been planned that Sam himself should discover the body. Accident had given Sam nearly the worst possible set of circumstances, but accidents cannot be planned; the crime had been expected to speak for itself, in Sam's absence. The killer, in short, could hardly have expected that Sam would be able to investigate before anyone else did.

It would be half an hour at the least, Sam estimated, before the first assistant professor or instructor would enter the building and at least an hour before the first undergraduate would be seeking Dr. Fred's lab and advice. Fifteen minutes should be enough to examine the sludge of papers before the open safe, and the opportunity justified almost any risk.

Sam pulled the sleeve of his jacket down over his left hand and slipped open the drawer where the gynecological equipment was kept. The rubber gloves were there, all right, but they were dulled by a thin film of dusting starch. Anything he touched with those would be marked. Yet he could not afford a fingerprint. He had never before touched Dr. Fred's records, and it would be important to leave no evidence that he had.

Again he decided in favor of the lesser risk. Use of the gloves would show, but it would not point, except to suggest that there might be fingerprints inside the tips of the gloves. He wished the forthcoming fingerprint experts joy of that problem, for without stopping to think he could name thirteen people who had worn those gloves within the past six months alone.

He used the gloves.

Sena's entire dossier was missing. So were those of Kelland, Hammy Saunders, Maurey, and Sam himself. In addition, random sections of other dossiers were, in his own fervent cliché, conspicuous by their absence. The names of the giants involved made a group in Sam's mind, but he could not quite label the group as yet, and he gave over trying for the moment. The absence of the papers on Sena's and his own cases was conclusive enough for his own purposes, since it enabled him to name to himself the name he had been crowding out of his consciousness up until now:

Maurice St. George.

Maurey, the chief god of all the stumbling Olympians Dr. Fred had produced, had rewarded his maker.

Sam closed his eyes for a long moment, overcome. Not murder; no; parricide. And cruelest of all was the awful impatience it showed. Dr. Fred had been going to die this year in any event—all his children knew that. But Maurey had been unable to wait.

And had he really needed Dr. Fred's death? That was impossible to guess, but Sam suspected not. In Maurey's mind it had probably been no more than a weapon to use against Sam—and in that puny cause the greatest mind and heart since Einstein's had been slaughtered like a pig.

Sam could appreciate the subtlety of the planting even better after that conclusion—and his own flash of guilt as well: to kill Dr. Fred to dispatch such an emmet as Sam Ettinger! The apparent crudity of the frame-up—for instance, the abandonment of the unique, easily ticketable weapon—would seem to rule out Maurey at once. Maurey

had done more than implicate Sam. He had staged the
scene to suggest a clumsy attempt to *fake* a frame-up. Sam
felt an iron-clad certainty that Maurey's efforts would not
go to waste. Maurey never did anything incompletely.

Was there anything more to take into consideration?
Yes—the dog.

There was the one remaining factor visible to Sam upon
which no plan could count. Maurey could not have dared
to kill the dog, and had not so dared, since it was known
among the giants that Decibelle did not like Maurey. Furthermore, Maurey was unsentimental, and would not have
thought of the dog at all except in terms of telltale torn
trousers. Instead, Sam surmised, he had worked quickly,
well above the level of the animal's understanding until it
was far too late; and then had left, before Decibelle had
been able to confirm Dr. Fred's death, or even the fact of
a quarrel. Very probably, in fact, there had been no quarrel, but an unexpected silent blast from the projector, a
crash of equipment, a heavy impact, footsteps receding in
the creaking stairwell—and a frightened, an abruptly and
puzzledly lonely dog.

But the dog was not stupid. It was not in any sense an
ordinary dog. Maurey had gotten away from his outrage
without being attacked—but there were now some matters
about which no doubt could exist in Decibelle's slow but
inexorably direct mind.

"Decibelle," Sam muttered. "Hey-pup. Where's Sena?
Where is she? Where's Sena?"

Decibelle looked up.

"Hey-pup. Hey Decibelle. Where's Sena? Find Sena. Go
find Sena."

The repetition told. The dog, her ears still drooping,
looked toward the door, and then back at Sam.

"That's right. Go find her. Go on. Go find Sena."

Decibelle thought about it, blinking her blood-shot eyes
alternately and rather upsettingly. Then she stood up, or
almost stood up, and crept back toward Dr. Fred.

"No, no. I'm here, puppy. I'll take care of Dr. Fred.
Don't you worry. Leave it to Sam. Get Sena. Come on,
Decibelle, find Sena. *Hey*-now. That's a good pup. Go to
Sena. Go find Sena."

The immense animal looked back at Sam.

"That's it, Decibelle. Sam's here. Go to Sena. *Come*-on,

Decibelle. Find Sena. Tell Sena about Maurey. You're a good girl, you did your job. Now tell Sena."

At the word "Maurey," the hair along the dog's spine coarsened. By the time Sam had come to his final order, Decibelle's back looked like a scrubbing-brush. Her claws ticking on the boards, she moved reluctantly toward the door.

"Hurry, Decibelle. That's it, that's it! Find Sena! Quick pup! Go get Sena!"

Suddenly, it took. The dog growled, softly, a sound as ragged and ugly for all its distance as the encounter of a buzz-saw with rusty metal. Instantly and without transition the great beast bayed, bayed enormous and bloody murder, and lunged out and down the stairs. The belling cry burst forth onto the campus and receded on the fresh morning air.

Sam listened to the dimming clamor for a moment. Then he swabbed his forehead with his wilted handkerchief, put away the rubber gloves and picked up Dr. Fred's phone. Now it no longer mattered if his fingers left prints.

"Susie? Sam Ettinger. Get me the police. Yes, please. No, don't ask any questions—keep your nose clean. The police—pronto."

The Civil Freedoms Association, an accredited undergraduate study club, met in the cellar of the Romance Languages house, in a moderately luxurious, cedar-panelled room which, though quite small, was usually too large for the group. Tonight, however, the attendance had turned out to be so large that the cellar clubroom was an impossibility. As the room became more jammed and the air still bluer with smoke, June—who was president this year—looked more and more worried, and Maurey, despite himself, more and more contented. Finally the meeting was adjourned upstairs to the house's largest classroom, where Spanish was taught during the day.

The reason, to nobody's surprise, was a turn-out in force of the tetras themselves—the diploid membership of the equal-rights bloc had never been much more than tiny. The crisis over Sam's killing of Dr. Fred had made a general conference unavoidable; and Maurey had agreed, reluctantly, with June that the giants' strongest diploid supporters should add their small encouragement and advice.

There were also a few policemen present, supposedly to
protect so large a gathering of giants and fellow-travellers
from being mobbed by a possibly outraged citizenry; their
number was small, but their publicity value was enormous.
(This suggestion, too, June had thought her own.) The
presence of the police, in turn, made newspaper reporters
inevitable.

The formal opening of the meeting was considerably
delayed while Maurey waited for the last possible giant to
appear. The rest of the tetras—mostly of the Titan faction
—twisted in their seats, like high school students crowded
under fourth-graders' desks by a building shortage, and
muttered to each other. The local Hearst reporter, who had
also to attend a Mothers' March on Cancer across town,
interviewed Maurey briefly without seeming to listen very
closely to his answers, and left.

Finally June caught Maurey's eye. He shrugged and
moved his fingers away from his chest as if trundling some
round object toward the edge of a table. June made a
smart tattoo with the gavel.

"Friends, let's get to the business at hand," she said
clearly above the thrum of talk. She looked extraordinarily
young on the rostrum. "I won't call the roll or fuss around
with parliamentarianisms tonight—this meeting is too important and we're starting rather late. I'm going to ask our
large confreres to sit quiet a while longer while we hear
from Tom Drobinski. Tom's editor of the Dunhill *Campus
Echo*, and the head of our public relations committee. I
think he can tell us something about what the public temper
is like right now. Shoot, Tom."

Drobinski, a swarthy sophomore journalism major with
a cranial structure that would have thrown a frog into
convulsions of jealousy, stood up and said rapidly:

"You've all seen most of the papers so I won't go into
detail on that. Briefly, they're all taking the same line, except the *Worker*, which hasn't taken any notice at all yet,
and the *Times*, which made a fairly successful try at being impartial.

"We haven't the facilities to do a complete monitoring
job as far as the air is concerned, but the videocasts I've
seen myself all played up the parricide angle, and used lots
of myth-faking and crude dream symbols—heavy emphasis
on mystery, hazy gigantic figures. Biblical references to

'giants in the Earth,' the kind of thing that makes people feel alarmed without knowing why. On the whole I think that everybody, but everybody, thinks Ettinger is guilty, except for some of the leftist columnists who *know* he's guilty but sort of wish he weren't. Some kind of identification reaction there, but I'm not analyst enough to make it very clear, even to myself."

"Give us a sample, Tommy," one of the diploids said.

"Well, Tex Warner has a long, quasi-Freudian chew in tonight's New York *Weathervane*, hinting that big people are just naturally murderous because nobody loves them, but that it's black Fascism to single them out. The piece is slugged 'First of a Series,' so I'm afraid the wisdom will get thicker before it gets thinner. But that's on the side. I saw a mess of news service dispatches from the capitol just before I came here. One of the state senators is going to put a resolution on the floor tomorrow to have the adult tetra colony taken back under state supervision, now that the University's yielded its jurisdiction—"

"But Tommy, that must be illegal!"

"No it isn't," Drobinski said. "The laws relating to Indian reservations haven't been needed for seventy years, but they're still on the books. That's only the beginning. There's another resolution being drafted to register all the tetras with the Habitual Offenders Monitor, give them numbers, make them show wallet cards to new employers, and all that. A spokesman for SPEECH—the Society for Prevention of Exploitation, *et cetera*—has announced that the Society will not associate itself in any way with or contribute any funds whatever to the defense of the accused. And there's going to be a lot more trouble tomorrow—Ira Methfessel has just announced a big spectacle of some kind, evidently the tournament that all the rumors have been about, and the stadium box office claims that people are already climbing all over each other to get tickets."

He stopped speaking as though he had been turned off, and sat down. Then his voice shot forth again from among the seats, startlingly.

"We're about two weeks away from Pasadena, I'd say," he declared with flat clarity. "Only this time—"

"June, may I chip in?"

The deep, gentle voice came into the tense silence like a benison. June smiled.

"We have to think about Sam right now," the speaker said from the back of the room. "Maurey, do you think he has a prayer of getting a fair trial?"

"Yes and no," Maurey said, rising. "Obviously there'll be political bias. It'll be impossible to pick a jury that won't already be largely anti-tetra, emotionally. Is that what you mean, Kelland?"

"Just that."

"Well, I see nothing that we can do about it. Except for that factor, I expect the trial to be scrupulously fair. Naturally, we'll have to get ourselves a good lawyer, as brilliant a man as our pooled resources can afford; we don't want to risk a court-appointed defense counsel in a matter as vital to us as this. I'm sure Methfessel will let us have an advance on the gate for the tournament if he's properly approached—"

There was a racket on the floor. The center of the disturbance was another giant, an Atlantean, who was now standing and shouting. Since there were four other giants shouting at him, Maurey, and each other at the same time, nothing coherent came through. June added the crack of the gavel to the din, which subsided promptly.

"What were you hollering, Briggs?"

"That it's ridiculous to talk about doing anything for Sam Ettinger," Briggs said hotly. "If he's so innocent, where's his girl?"

"She's not a member of the Civil Freedoms Association," said Maurey, coldly.

"Hardly anybody else here is, either. You can't excuse her on those grounds. But everybody who—one way or the other—gives a damn what happens to Sam Ettinger managed to attend this meeting. Except Sena Carlin."

Maurey hung his head for a second and went so far as to shuffle his feet a little. He could not remember ever having needed to use the appearance of embarrassment and indecision before, but it seemed ridiculously easy. He made a temporizing noise and liked it so well he made it again. "Uhmm," he said. "Uhmmmmm."

He fell silent, in the full knowledge that Sena was ensconced in Dr. Fred's cabin, unapproachable because she had taken that damned dog with her, and that the two of them were mourning Dr. Fred. He let the momentary silence grow and swell. Then, with an air of fumbling avoidance of the truth, he said, "Sena has friends as well as a husband, Briggs. Maybe she wouldn't enjoy being in the public eye just now. Maybe she's in a kind of seclusion—"

"She's gone straight to Polly Follmer's, hasn't she?" asked an anonymous female voice, so sure of the answer that it wasn't really a question, but an indictment. The name echoed, like corn in the popper when the oil reaches a certain heat: *Polly Polly Polly Polly.*

Maurey wondered why he was doing this to Sena, but he did not have time enough to stop and sort out his intentions. He allowed a look of intense guilt to convulse his face, wiped it off, and perfectly deadpan quashed the inference while underscoring it. "I didn't say that," he said tonelessly.

"You don't have to say it. I say it," said Briggs. "And that makes it doubly ridiculous to talk about doing anything for Sam Ettinger. Here his wife goes off with her loose-living friends, giving us a further bad name, as soon as he goes and creates this stink. What he's done makes him as vicious an enemy of ours as the kept press. If we band together behind him, the public will identify us with him. What we should do is draft a resolution condemning the murder, and demanding quick, merciless justice; pass it unanimously, and give it to the reporters."

"That's the stuff to give the troops," an excitable diploid crowed.

"I have nothing against mercy myself," Maurey said mildly. "And neither one resolution nor twenty is going to speed up justice any faster than the law will let it go."

"The words don't matter. The important thing is to dissociate ourselves from Ettinger."

"Throw out the Jonah," Kelland suggested.

Briggs failed to take the remark as a criticism, or even to place the metaphor.

"Exactly; throw him to the wolves," he growled, deporting the sea-faring Jonah to a droshky with a single stroke. "He's earned it. What he's done is—it's untetraploid, that's what. He's a Pasadentist."

"What was done was bad," Maurey said, unruffled. "But we have absolutely no proof that Sam did it. That's for the court to decide. He designed the weapon that was used, to the best of my knowledge, but I myself put the weapon into Dr. Fred's safe, and there's no direct evidence that Sam got it out again, or that he even knew the combination."

"I'm not sure he designed that gadget," Kelland interrupted. "I've worked on things of that type myself, from specifications you gave me, Maurey."

There was a flurry of scribbling among the reporters. Maurey frowned warningly, but Kelland plunged on.

"You have my drawings and could have built a projector yourself to my design," he said. "Hell, Maurey, nobody even knows whether or not the gadget really was the murder weapon. A young male giant could easily crush a frail old man's chest in an identical fashion with the back of a shovel, in one swipe."

"There was no shovel found," Maurey said coldly.

"I know that. Naturally there wouldn't have been, if the projector was just a blind."

Maurey stared at the huge man crammed like a retarded adolescent into a child's desk, and felt himself helplessly going white-lipped. He had always suspected that Kelland was not very bright, but this was abusing the privilege.

Since he could not control the emotional reaction, however, he would have to account for it before some dangerous construction was put upon it. The easiest and quickest way was to take offense.

"Pardon me, Kelland," he said, "but it's a good thing I know you well and know that you're a blunt and sometimes blundering sort of guy socially. Otherwise I might have to lose my temper. Everything you say is true, but it could also be taken to add up to an accusation—of murder. Not a very thoughtful thing to do in public."

"I'm sorry," Kelland said at once. "I have no intention of accusing you, God knows. I simply wanted to point out that Briggs is hanging Sam well in advance of any proof that he's done anything wrong."

"The point," Maurey said, "is well taken, if badly put. What about that, Briggs?"

Briggs' opinion was succinct but unprintable.

"I demand a vote," he added.

"On what?"

"On whether or not we denounce Ettinger. What else?"

"Will you go along with the decision if it goes against you?" Maurey asked curiously.

"Sure; what do you take me for? *Whatever* we do, it ought to be unanimous. You're asking so many questions, let me ask you one: who do *you* think murdered Dr. Fred?"

Timed to the split second, Maurey thought with secret admiration.

"It's not my function to decide that," Maurey said, making each word tell. "However, Briggs, I seriously doubt that any tetra would have raised a hand against the old man, whatever the fancied or real provocation. If we do decide to help defend Sam, part of our effort ought to go also toward looking elsewhere."

There had been a murmuring of side-chatter all through the meeting, a murmur of private debates whose participants could not afford more than one ear for the discussion. Now, as the iron in Maurey's speech began to bite deeper, the room became more and more quiet, until at last there was an unearthly silence. The reporters bent intently over their notebooks and wads of yellow copy-paper, and Maurey could see in his mind's eye the rewrite men conceiving the headlines:

LUMMOXES HINT NON-GIANT SLEW
DR. HYATT; THREATEN VENDETTA

But he wanted those headlines to surprise the tetras, so he did not dare let the silence persist long enough for full comprehension to set in.

"June," he said, "would you rend some paper in twain and pass out the tatters? If you favor hiring a lawyer for Sam, friends, write 'Yes,' and drop the slips in the hat as usual. If the 'No' slips predominate, we'll entertain a new motion."

But, of course, the Yesses won. There were two 'No' votes. One was Maurey's own; Briggs himself had agreed to cast the other one to keep in character, and Maurey was more than glad of the fore-planning. He had not anticipated such a landslide.

He announced the results. The reporters broke for the door. Maurey looked at Briggs, who shrugged.

The shrug was a genuine artistic stroke. Briggs would become a great actor in the new world, Maurey thought, if he lived to see it.

Maurey was in honest doubt as to whether or not he should.

IX

Sam had found with dull astonishment what every newly-imprisoned man finds: that after only a brief isolation from his own world, he could no longer understand the news. He read through the local paper's lead-story account of the "conference of war" with the conviction that none of the tetras whose names were attached to the quotations could have said anyhing like that; yet, as a whole, the story hung together.

There was a great deal more that was puzzling. Methfessel had announced his tournament—there was a half-page ad for it in the sports section, and a quarter of the editorial copy in the section was devoted to it. Methfessel's ad made very little sense, in as many type-style as a 19th Century American theater poster:

"SEE Titans in Deadly Combat! SEE Flying Shock Troops Clash in Mid-Air! SEE Affairs of Honor FOUGHT TO THE FINISH with SWORDS OF FIRE! Towering Heroes Contend for the Favors of Gorgeous Giantesses with Strange Weapons *never before used on any battlefield!* Champions in Armor—Mass Charges—Futuristic Warfare—Blazing Color, Beauty, Spectacle! THE EVENT OF A LIFETIME!" And more, proving nothing that Sam could see but that Barnum was not dead after all.

The sportswriters were generally hostile, or, at the least, sarcastic, but appeared to have little better idea of what Methfessel actually planned than Sam could deduce. Certainly the propoganda hardly suggested mailed knights on brewery horses, despite the medieval trappings of the ad-writer's copy.

On the editorial page, the newspaper's proprietors took a dim view of the whole business, suggesting darkly that there was something frivolous—in another century the editorial might have said "worldly"—in the giants' staging a circus when their whole existence was a matter of the gravest concern among right-thinking normal human beings. Like most editorialists, however, the writer seemed to fear standing too strongly on one side of the fence, despite not having to sign his name; for the editorial wound up with a foggily hopeful remark about people putting their best feet forward. Perhaps this was intended to pass for impartiality.

The smaller stories about the crime itself were a little more comprehensible. Sena, who had been held as a material witness, had been released upon a stiff bail which Maurey had put up (Sam had thus far been unable to speak to her). The paper had a "human interest" interview with her, which wavered nervously between the straight sob-sister treatment and a tendency toward acidulousness. There was no mention of the dog, for which Sam was grateful no matter what it meant.

The trial date was already set, a two-column italic headline announced. A box on page 12 contained an irrelevant datum about Sam's University post, evidently supposed to be funny. There was a column of fuzzily learned speculation about the weapon, written by the man who usually did the paper's "Weekly Walks With Nature"—Maurey had declined to explain the mechanism except before the grand jury, on the grounds that there was a patent pending on the principle which publication of details would prejudice. Finally, there was a meandering roundup yarn dealing with official reactions to the murder, including the news of Sam's dismissal from the graduate faculty— apparently there was pressure from the alumni association to dismiss all the tetras from such posts, but the Dunhill board was still standing fast at the moment—and a comment from the state's governor which "promised prompt punishment for provocative acts."

All of which was alarming without being in the least enlightening. What most irritated Sam—his strongest emotion now, for it was impossible to sustain an intense consciousness of personal danger continuously for a week, or a sense of personal outrage at invisible persons—was his being cast, at this point, for the role of the Impotent Husband in a bad videocast. The stage was all set for the Big Think, wherein the male lead was to take a long walk or be shut up in a room until he Came-to-Realize, with his own voice squawking at him through a filter (representing Thoughts) to a background of treacly organ-music.

The irritation, of course, sprang from the fact that a

Big Think was by this time a commodity for which Sam
had no use. He had Come-to-Realize a week ago, in a
split second, without benefit of filtered voices or *vox
humana tremolo*. Sam's thinking was often slow, but his
conclusions were usually none the less sound for being be-
lated. He knew, he was certain, the name of Dr. Fred's
murderer, and he knew in general what Maurey's purpose
had to be: to widen the gap between giants and diploids
by every subtle means, and to provoke an eventual break
in which Pasadena would happen again—*in the opposite
direction*, with the giants the victors, the diploids the elim-
inated.

Sam had been blind to the implications of the one-way
push as a weapon, but his was a type of mind that saw
things at once upon demonstration, and did not need to
be shown twice. Jolted into thinking of the phenomenon
in military terms, he could envision half a dozen expedients—side-arms, pressor fields, an anti-missile field—any
one of which he could have designed with a minimum of
experimentation. On a very large scale, with a sufficient
set of receptors, even an anti-fusion bomb field was possible, one which would scale its resistance exactly to the
output—or the distance—of the explosion.

From this point of view Maurey's apparently suicidal
program appeared in a different and much grimmer light,
and reminded Sam that a hundred men who knew the basic
uses of explosives could have taken over the Roman Em-
pire by direct frontal attack. Things were not so simple
now; Maurey's program was still suicidal, but the size of
the expectable casualty list grew every time Sam considered another implication.

Maurey had called the tournaments a blind for his Moon
colonization project. It was interesting to see what revelations could come out of standing Maurey's statements on
their heads. Maurey had never had the faintest interest in
the Moon, as Sam knew he should have seen at once. On
the other hand, it was now clear that the tournaments were
essential—that they were nothing less than training grounds
for a tetraploid militia, for training in a new and terrifying
armamentarium.

But it was in the matter of the "phony" tetraploidy that
Maurey's massive intelligence had shone most brilliantly.
Sam had a sickening hunch that there actually was some-

thing—amiss—in Sena's genetic background, but Maurey's moves made sense all down the line even if one assumed that the whole "phony" story had been pure invention. The accusation had invalidated Sam out of any participation in anti-diploid politics, a field where Maurey could not afford to trust him: first by giving Sam something more immediate to think about, and second by providing the other giants with grounds for sharing Maurey's distrust of Sam.

The murder followed logically. It stowed Sam safely away physically, as the "phony" story had already isolated him politically; and at the same time it multiplied anti-diploid feeling marvelously by making martyrs of both victim and accused at once. Finally, the records which had been taken from the safe had been selected with perfect cunning to suggest that the very tetras who were least likely to go along with Maurey's plans were also "phony" in their genetic makeup—and that Maurey himself might belong to that genetic group, which made *him* look like the same altruist they had been trusting all along.

It had been well done. Sam, lying full length on the cell bunk with his arms folded under his head and his feet on the cold floor, was surprised to find in himself an impersonal streak which found it all admirable. None of his deductions had thrown him into the expectable fury against Maurey. The renegade giant, in Sam's limited philosophical vocabulary, simply had no morals.

Maurey was also something of a philosopher; he had had practice at it. Here, perhaps, was where his greatest advantage over his adversaries had lain all along. He, and he alone, had known enough about what he was doing to think about it in philosophical terms, and to formulate—for purposes of counter-action—how people of opposing philosophies might view the problem, at their best. In the eyrie of his solitary brain, Maurey had been doing all the thinking for both sides until recently, and Maurey knew more than enough of the "minimax" policy of the theory of games to credit his opponents always with their best possible strategy—which was far better than they would actually be likely to do for themselves, having entered the game this late and this full of ignorance.

And yet he was already beginning to violate the rules, for nobody with Maurey's basic view of the game could play it canny forever, sheerly to maximize his gains and minimize his losses. There was another goal in view than that; and where the goal was concerned, Maurey was not a minimax player, but a fanatic.

No, he was neither mad nor bad; only a direct-actionist, as expedient as a woman. He was a social outcast like all the tetras, but he was unlike them in following exile into its last ditch—that murky declivity where there is no such thing as bad means. Maurey could not believe that bad means corrupt good ends, nor that his ends might be bad as well.

This trait in Maurey Sam had seen often in the laboratory, where there are no moral problems; usually with the result that Gordian knots fell asunder with Alexandrine suddennness. Early in the study of the one-way push, Sam had resisted a suggested line of inquiry on the ground that it was mathematically ridiculous. His chief had said:

"Are you going or staying, Sam? Math is just rationalization after the deed. If you're going, then go, and let the explanations wait. If you don't want to go, then stay home, but don't complain that the goal you've abandoned doesn't show on the map. If you've decided to stay home, you don't care what the map shows. The place you *want* to go to always exists until proven otherwise—even if the maps mark it 'Terra Incognita' or 'Here Are Dragons.' "

Maurey was admirable. Nevertheless, living as a human being demanded a constant fight for protection against his logical kind. Sam had personal objections to mangling the lives of others for any end; and the same impersonality that allowed him to admire Maurey's clarity, his brilliance, his impatient cutting through the various traps and rituals of standard scientific method, made him ruthless against the ends Maurey sought. It would make him equally ruthless against Maurey himself, when the time came.

He thought that time was coming, but he knew that he had hardly a noticeable fraction of Maurey's intricacy. All he had to go on was a dubious faith, not a surety, and not even a glimpse of what the outcome might be.

There were footsteps outside, and Sam propped himself up on one elbow. The guards were bringing him his dinner.

By diploid standards the guards were tough and chunky animals, as formidable as bears. But then, by diploid standards the bars of Sam's cell were impassible, while against Sam they had to be electrified.

The guards put Sam's tray on the floor before the door and backed off to either side, retrieving their shotguns. Both of them looked up toward a point well over Sam's head, their faces lit weakly by the red bulb which, Sam had already decided, showed whether the current in the bars was on or off. Then the glow vanished from their stubbly dewlaps and they looked down again. One of them picked up the tray and shoved it through the slot in the cagework—a slot only just large enough to pass a diploid's head if he jammed it through sideways, without caring about what happened to his ears. It would pass Sam's flat hand, but not his fist.

"Come and get it, lummox."

Sam got up and bent to pull the tray through the bars. As usual, the meal was heavy, more than double the ration for the biggest possible diploid, and so nearly double what Sam needed. His katabolic rate, like that of all the giants, was very slow, and a high proportion of what he ate served him as fuel rather than as material for the building of new cells. Evidently the prison authorities had assumed that he'd been returning his meals half uneaten because he'd been too nervous to clean the plates.

It was only one more sign that the people who had the best reasons to be concerned with the problem of the tetraploids had not made the smallest effort to learn the available facts about them, though all the facts had been available for half a century.

The guards watched, waiting for the light to come on again. They were stupid, but not unfriendly, despite the gingerly way in which they had to approach him.

"Heard the news?" one of them said.

"I saw the morning paper," Sam said, denuding a chop-bone. "Something's come up since?"

"The gov'ner's put the kibosh on the big show you guys was going to stage," the guard said. "Says it might cause a riot. What was it going t' be like, anyhow? Was you rilly going t' fly through the air an' all that?"

"I wish I knew," Sam said. "I got clapped in here before I heard more than a rumor or two. Methfessel seems to have changed his plans since then."

"It's a damn dirty trick, if you ast me," the other guard said. The light came on, and they lowered their guns and came a little closer to the door. "I bought tickets for the wife an' kids—two bucks a throw for seats way up in the bleachers. This Messfettel going t' give refunds or rain-checks or like that?"

"Oh, sure," Sam said. "He'd have to. He's been running the sports for the University up to now—I'm pretty sure he's honest."

"Well, the family's going t' be pissed off about missing it, all the same."

"You was lucky," the first guard grumbled. "They wasn't no tickets when *I* got t' the box-office. I got mine from a scalper at ten rocks a throw. One buck seats, too. I'm gonna lose nine apiece on 'em, an' a couple the other boys is in the same fix. If I had this Missfussel I'd take it outa his hide—but I guess it ain't his fault, neither. But it ain't as if I got money t' burn."

"Tough," Sam said sincerely. "As far as I'm concerned, I don't think Methfessel had any business announcing the tournament to begin with. He should have known it'd just have made more trouble."

Of course, he realized, the cancellation wouldn't hurt Ira's future gates a bit, provided that he could get the prohibition lifted in due course.

"Yeah," the guard said, rather automatically, since it was obvious that he hadn't been listening. "Looked like it was going t' be good, too. Every onct in a while we could see one of the big guys shooting up above the stadium and down again like a freaking eagle—"

"You could see—!"

"Just accidental," the guard said hastily. "Not that we was snooping. We paid our money fair an' square, so why should we of snooped?"

"Oh, I didn't mean that," Sam said. But it was impossible to admit what he had meant by his interjection—he was almost afraid even to think about it before an audience. His appetite extinguished suddenly, he put his tray back on the ledge and slid it out. The guards, shrugging at his sudden reticence, took it up and went off.

Sam sat still on the narrow bunk, chill and stunned. So the talk about flying in Methfessel's ad hadn't been just hyperbole! Evidently Maurey, perhaps with help, had developed the one-way push into a sort of—well, a sort of bootstrap for self-lifting purposes. Of course it was now easy to see how such a thing could be designed—but Sam

hadn't seen it before, all the same. Evidently he had
needed the Big Think much more than he'd been ready to
believe.

Sam thought some more.

After he was through thinking, he was still sitting on the
bunk. This fact could not be thought away; it was the
most important thing he had to think about. If Maurey
had any sort of flying equipment—and even a "flying belt"
was not unthinkable—he would without doubt stage some
sort of melodramatic rescue raid on the prison where Sam
was held. Not because he wanted Sam out—far from it—
but because it suited his other purposes ideally.

Sam found that pill hard to swallow, but he swallowed it.
The subtleties of amoral persons, of "expedient" politics,
invariably wound up in just such cataclysmic crudities if
they were pushed far enough along the line of their own
logic, and Maurey was exactly the man to push that far.
Maurey was a genius in most respects, true, but his ability
to boggle at the verge of disaster was slightly below that
of a lemming.

And no amount of thinking would turn up any more
logical specific step than that of a raid on the jail. No
other percussion-cap for a showdown-by-force with the
diploids could be expected to crop up for some years longer
than Maurey's patience could be expected to last. All Maurey's plans pointed to exactly that—indeed they were ulti-
mately explicable only in terms of that intent and no other.

The raid could only precipitate a massacre. In the confusion Sam would perhaps get away, and afterward he
would have to be shown to the tetras who had freed him;
that meant that he probably would not be killed treacher-
ously under the guise of being done a favor. The chances
were slightly less good for Sena, for if there were hidden
in her any solution to the tetraploid problem, however dis-
agreeable, Maurey would have to know it in its totality in
order to combat it, as that same knowledge would be
needed to make it work.

In both cases, there would remain some question as to
who was supposed to be exterminating whom, until the
very last poor dog was hung, and the remaining bloody
noses counted. But for now, Sam had only one function
in the drama:

He sat and waited.

X

Sam's lawyer was young, short of stature, and implacably cheerful. His name was Wlodzmierzc, a Polish ghetto corruption of "Weltschmerz"—the kind of name newspapers never misspell (the Andresons and the Smithes are the unhappy cognomens which get ignored by the proofreader). Wlodzmierzc was chatting with the reporters now, as had been his practice during the past three days toward the end of every recess, switching effortlessly into one or another of six different languages as needed, none of them his own.

The additional languages were always needed, for the world press had taken up the story of the trial, and legal observers from the International Court of Justice also were present. Wlodzmierzc himself was a union appointee who had presented his credentials to Maurey before Maurey had decided on a man in whom to invest the tetras' warchest. Since the Pole was obviously better qualified than any possible lawyer Maurey could have hired, and since in addition none of the tetras could afford to give away money where there was no need, Maurey had been forced to pass the sums back to the original contributors.

Whether or not Maurey had been happy about this remained an open question. He had not confided in Sam. The imprisoned giant suspected, however, that Maurey had accepted it as an accomplished fact, and therefore not worth more than a mild swearword or two.

Even Sam himself had seen it coming, as soon as the Soviet UN delegation, still smarting from their government's having been forced by ICJ review to return five acquittals in the Belgrade trials, had suggested the possibility of "lynch law in the American giant case."

Even the American representatives had had to admit that "some public prejudice might possibly affect the conduct of the trial," in particular after a prior admission that since no Federal crime was involved, the FBI had taken no interest and the case would be tried before the court of the county in which Dunhill University was located; and that some of the provisions of law involved had been unchanged in that state since 1766. After that, though the way to be traversed had still been tortuous, a Wlodzmierzc had been clearly visible at its end.

The bailiff rapped, and the lawyer came back quickly to the defense table, smiling innocently at Sam.

"Anything new?" the giant said in a low voice. The lawyer seated himself and leaned sidewise; always, when seated, he watched the bench and the witness chair and the jury box steadfastly, never looking at Sam, but canting alarmingly whenever they had to speak.

"Not very much, I am afraid. I am beginning to feel that international intervention here has had a largely ugly effect upon the local populace, and such an attitude inevitably will filter through to the jury and perhaps even to the judge. A pity that the ICJ wouldn't grant us a change of venue to England."

"I wish you'd explain again why you tried that."

"A question of publicity purely, Sam. English law does not permit newspapers, television commentators or any other part of the press to discuss a criminal case until a decision has been handed down. Afterwards they may give complete accounts of the trial, and claim abuses of justice if they believe they have seen any, but beforehand, no. The UN's proposed World Code includes such a provision, but the United States and several other—" He dropped abruptly into the telegraphic pidgin he used while the court was actually in session. "No matter now. Here's judge. Be brave."

"Sena Hyatt Carlin!" the bailiff cried.

The audience stirred. This was to be its first chance to look in person on the "Blonde Princess," the "Titans' Daughter," who had been featured so prominently in the tabloid accounts. Sena came to the stand confidently, was sworn in, turned, and sat down with a concentrated grace. Her expression was clear, and a little cold—suggesting neither disgust nor contempt, but simply aloofness. Sam took a deep, quiet breath.

Both the aloofness and the confidence became more marked as she answered the preliminary questions. They came rapidly, and Sena answered them at the same pace, using the number of words proper to answer the question as put, no more, no less, allowing the district attorney to establish her identity and her qualifications as a witness. Technically she was on cross-examination, since she was a defense witness, but a peculiarity in Wlodzmierzc's procedure, apparently deliberate, had allowed Sturm first crack at her. In the same position Sam would have gone slowly, wary of possible traps in the first routine queries, but Sena did not appear to be afraid; and when it was over, Wlodzmierzc nodded once to himself.

The prosecutor might have been impressed, if unwillingly, by her self-possession; in any event he set no traps. He said at last:

"Now, Miss Carlin, is it true that the late Dr. Hyatt never informed you that you were not a tetraploid individual?"

"No."

"No, he did not?"

"No, it is not true," Sena said.

"Then he *did* so inform you?"

"No. He had no true information of that kind to give."

The D.A. smiled.

"We'll let that pass for the moment. You have read Dr. St. George's testimony—I refer to that part of his deposition in which a visit by him to the dormitory room of the accused is described. Is that description accurate to the best of your knowledge?"

"Quite accurate," Sena said coldly, "as far as it goes."

"Very good, let's raise that question at once. Did you, at the time of that conversation, believe that Dr. St. George might have been misleading you as to the facts? Misleading you deliberately?"

"No. No, I didn't."

"Quite," the prosecutor said in succulent tones. "You considered, then; that there might be a real barrier, or let us say an impediment, to your having children by the accused?"

For the first time, Sena appeared to be slightly uncertain.

"I suppose I did feel that way," she said at last. "For the most part, though, I was just alarmed, and—well, anxious to find out whether Maur—whether Dr. St. George was right."

"I will not protest that answer, but I will ask you in the future to confine youself more closely to the question proper," the D. A. said. "Now—"

Wlodzmierzc snapped open like an automatic card table. "Objection."

The judge looked interestedly at the Pole, as one examines one's first fossil dinosaur egg. Wlodzmierzc said, "Miss Carlin answered Mr. Sturm's question, your honor. Thereafter she is entitled to explain her answer at whatever lengh your honor thinks pertinent; this is not a matter on which Mr. Sturm is entitled to rule."

"I am sure Mr. Sturm knows that, Mr. Wlodzmierzc."

"Granted. I ask only your honor's agreement, since the jury may not know it."

"Well, the jury knows it now. Anything else? Proceed, Mr. Sturm."

The D. A. sighed pityingly at Wlodzmierzc and turned back to Sena. Something that under any other circumstances would have been a leer subtly altered his expression. "Now, Miss Carlin: Prior to Dr. St. George's disclosure, you were 'married'—by the Williamsite ceremony —to the accused. He is your third common-law husband. Is that correct?"

"Objection! My honorable opponent's question is so phrased as to open the question of the family system among the tetraploid people. Such material would be irrelevant and most certainly prejudicial."

"The prejudicial aspects are clear," the judge admitted, turning to the prosecutor. There was a slight edge on his voice, and Sam was instantly convinced that the jury had been meant to notice it. "Mr. Sturm, are you prepared to defend the relevancy of the material?"

"No, your honor; my phrasing was fortuitous. With your permission I will withdraw the question and restate it."

Yeah, Sam thought glumly. Now that the jury has been reminded of what a loose-living crowd the lummoxes are anyhow—

"Yes, that's true," Sena was saying, white-lipped.

"Thank you. What was the reaction of the accused to Dr. St. George's disclosure?"

"He didn't believe it," Sena said.

"Quite; but Dr. St. George's deposition also says that the accused was angry. Was that your impression as well?"

"No," Sena said. "Anyhow, not exactly. Do you mean whether or not he seemed angry at Dr. Fred?"

The lawyer bowed ironically. "That is what I meant, Miss Carlin."

Sena shook her head. "Then, no. He didn't. He was upset, just as I was, but he couldn't be mad at Dr. Fred until he'd found out whether or not the story was true."

"Then he *would* have been angry had the victim told him the story was true?"

"That would depend upon the explanation, I should think. If Sam were shown a good reason for such a deception, I'm sure he'd go along."

"This is, however, merely your estimate of the defendant's character."

"Yes. That is what you asked me for, Mr. Sturm."

"Hmm. True. Very well. When did you first learn of the murder, Miss Carlin?"

"That morning. I think it was about seven o'clock."

Sturm smiled. "One hour after the accused's appointment with Dr. Hyatt, if I am not in error. And Mr. Ettinger notified you himself, I believe? Can you remember his exact words?"

"The first thing he said?"

"That will do nicely."

"Yes," Sena said. "He said, 'Check, Sena.'"

The D. A.'s smile turned magically into a scowl. "That's all?"

"Well, he said 'Good-bye,' too."

"Do you and Mr. Ettinger play much chess?"

"No. I don't know how. I have the impression that he does, but I don't think he's at all devoted to the game or plays it often. It's not really something we've ever talked about except in passing."

"But I presume you knew what the accused meant by, 'Check, Sena.'"

"I thought I knew."

"You're being rather unresponsive, Miss Carlin. Must I ask you directly what your opinion is of the meaning of 'Check, Sena'? Very well, I so ask: What *is* your opinion?"

"He meant to ask me to check the genetic aspects of

Dr. St. George's allegation. He saw, of course, that he was sure to be arrested and so would be in no positaion to check the matter further himself."

"Does it strike you that there are much simpler ways of interpreting the remark?"

Sam clutched Wlodzmierzc by the elbow, but the lawyer shook his head.

"Under the circumstances, no."

"Then will you explain, please, how two enigmatic words would suffice to inform you of a murder, unless it had been foreplanned in your presence?"

There was a long-drawn *a-a-a-a-ah* in the courtroom, general but too soft for any but the most conscientious judge to silence.

Sena said, "I already knew about the murder. Mr. Ettinger sent for me and I saw the body before *any* words were spoken at all. After that, not many words were needed."

"But surely he spoke words over the telephone?" Sturm said gently.

"No. He didn't telephone. He sent a friend."

"But with what message?

"No message."

"The friend simply appeared? And that was enough? If you please! Who *was* this friend?"

"Dr. Hyatt's dog."

The attorney turned bright crimson in the space of a second. "Miss Carlin," he said in a tight voice, "are you asking this court to believe that Mr. Ettinger managed to get you to come to Dr. Hyatt's laboratory merely by sending a dog after you? Or did he pin a tearful note to the dog's collar? Or was it, perhaps, a talking dog?"

"Which of your questions shall I answer?" Sena demanded angrily.

"None, Miss Carlin. None. I withdraw the questions. Mr. Wlodzmierzc, your witness." The prosecutor made such a triumphal march of going back to his table that Sam could almost hear strains of Meyerbeer in the stale air.

"One moment, Mr. Wlodzmierzc," the judge said nervously. "You realize, I'm sure, that you may object to the final line of questioning before taking the witness, under American law? I am not suggesting that the prosecution's questions were in any way improper, but I wish to be sure that the defense does not unknowingly forfeit any—"

"Thank you, your honor, but I have no objections to enter," Wlodzmierzc said in a brisk voice. "I am pleased that my learned opponent brought up this question of the dog. Miss Carlin, rather than consume more of the court's time bringing this information out piecemeal, I am going to make a brief statement about the dog myself; I shall then ask you whether or not the statement is correct, and if not, wherein it is in error."

"I object!" Sturm said hotly. "Your honor, surely the attorney of the accused is in no position to testify on behalf of a witness."

"He has a clear right to pose a hypothetical question," the judge said, "depending upon its content, of course. Proceed, Mr. Wlodzmierzc."

"Thank you, your honor. Miss Carlin, this is my formulation:

"The dog in question is a giant dog. It is not a tetraploid, but closely related to the tetraploids, in a theoretical sense. As such, it is of abnormal intelligence, as well as of abnormal size. It was this dog, then, which awoke you shortly before seven on the morning of the murder—to adopt my learned friend's way of referring to a day during which no such murder may have occurred—"

"Objection!"

"Overruled," the judge said unhappily.

"But your honor, the grand jury returned a true bill of murder—otherwise we should all not be here!"

"Mr. Wlodzmierzc didn't question that. He questioned the day."

"—by entering your dormitory building, pushing your door open, and pulling the covers off your bed. We have testimony to show that this dog, this same dog, was seen and heard on the campus at this time, being very noisy; however, it made no sound while in the dormitory."

"Are you prepared to substantiate this in any other way than by the passive agreement of the witness, Mr. Wlodzmierzc?"

"Yes, your honor. We are prepared to bring the animal here, and to demonstrate that it can follow complex directions, understand situations involving as many as three variables, and exercise reasoning faculties in general which are slightly greater than those of a chimpanzee, particularly those faculties which might be termed integrative. I may go so far as to say that this dog is one of the most important exhibits for the defense. In the meantime, however, I ask only that my statement be accepted as testimony from the *present* witness by virtue of whatever agreement she may vest in it."

"All right. Let's hear the rest."

"The rest is quickly told. Miss Carlin, you went with the dog to Dr. Hyatt's laboratory; she led you there. Once arrived, you found Mr. Ettinger and the body. Mr. Ettinger pointed to the spilled papers which have been mentioned before in this court, and said, 'Check, Sena.' You thereupon looked at all the papers during the next five minutes, and left that laboratory with the dog. At this point let me ask you whether or not I have stated the facts correctly."

"Quite correctly, Mr. Wlodzmierzc."

"Good." Wlodzmierzc darted with a sudden, sparrow-like movement to the defense table and returned, bearing a sheet of paper. "Your honor, I have here a sheet of paper of ordinary legal length, eleven and a half by fourteen inches. It is completely covered, as these warranted duplicates will show, by single-spaced, typewritten lines, ungrouped, which consist entirely of figures from a standard set of tables of random numbers; we will offer the book in evidence also.

"We prepared this document in the hope of providing something which could not possibly be memorized in advance by any ordinary person; Miss Carlin, in any event, has never seen it before and will so swear. Will the court allow us to show it to her for four seconds by stop-watch, in order to demonstrate that she is able to memorize it with complete accuracy in that time?"

"Well, Mr. Sturm?"

There followed one of those long, mumbled colloquies at the bench which never turn up in fiction or drama, but which may consume more than half the time of an actual trial, or even settle it before it starts. During the conference Sam was vaguely surprised to find himself in the throes of a chill of malarial violence. At last Sturm agreed to let Wlodzmierzc proceed with the demonstration, providing that Sena would also memorize in an additional four seconds two pages of the FAO world rice-production tables for 1948, to be selected by Sturm.

Sena did beautifully with both, muffing (as Wlodzmierzc had before the trial insisted that she should) eight of the thousand figures on the prepared sheet, and throwing in a stumble over one word in a footnote to the FAO tables for good measure. Neither Sena nor Sam had seen any reason for this, but Wlodzmierzc had taken the position that a perfect performance would be more suspect and hence less useful than a slightly flawed one.

"We have arranged this demonstration, your honor," the Pole said, "in order to establish that Miss Carlin is capable of memorizing written information in great quantities, practically instantaneously. Miss Carlin, will you confirm?"

"I have what is often called an eidetic memory, or total recall," Sena said composedly.

"And, Miss Carlin, did you so memorize the contents of Dr. Hyatt's papers while you were in the laboratory with the accused?"

"Yes, sir," Sena said. "There was plenty of time for that; I believe I went through them three times to make sure I had seen everything."

"Your honor, these papers are in evidence. If the court or the defense so wishes, Miss Carlin is prepared to quote at length from any given page as a further check."

The judge looked at Sturm, who shook his head. Wlodzmierzc said:

"The reason why we have been at pains to establish this fact will appear in a moment. Now, Miss Carlin, I am going to ask you a very important question, and I want you to consider your answer most carefully. This is the question: Did you, or did you not, see anything in those papers relating to your presumed non-tetraploid status?"

"That's very easy, Mr. Wlodzmierzc. I did."

"According to what you saw, are you a tetraploid individual?"

"No, sir."

The crowd murmured, but Wlodzmierzc was by no means through. "Is the accused?"

"No, sir."

"Is Dr. St. George?"

"Objection!" Sturm said. "Dr. St. George is not on trial. The question invades his right of privacy."

"Sustained," said the judge.

"Very well. Let me ask you this, Miss Carlin: Of the entire colony of giants, how many, according to your information, are tetraploid individuals?"

"None," Sena said flatly.

There was a roar of incredulous amazement in the court. The judge made no attempt to control it. After it had died down, however, he said, "Mr. Wlodzmierzc, almost I suspect you of provoking that statement sheerly for confusion's sake."

"Not guilty, your honor; the testimony is extremely relevant. Miss Carlin, does the accused know this fact—that is, had he known it up to this moment?"

"No, sir, not to my knowledge. I believe no one knew it but Dr. Hyatt's personal assistants, anud even among them it was customary to refer to us as 'tetras.'"

"Why was it?"

"Well, just because it was convenient, they tell me. Since every one of us has a different degree of polyploidy, and of a different kind, some overall handle was needed. The only other choice would have been 'Polly.'"

"I see. What, in your opinion, is the source of the confusion?"

"In the use of the term 'diploid' for people of 'normal' genetic constitution. The 'normal' human being actually is a *tetraploid* individual, like the tomato and certain other—"

This time the judge did pound for order, looking both baffled and wrathful.

"—but the doubling of the chromosomes apparently happened millenia ago, so that geneticists customarily speak of redoubled humans as tetras because they've twice the normal number of chromosomes. Actually, of course, such an individual would be an octoploid—like the giant strawberries you sometimes see on the market, the USDA Crimsons." She smiled. "Except that there are only two such individuals in our colony, we might have been nicknamed 'octopusses,' I suppose."

"Thank you. Your honor, we are of course now on redirect, but I feel that this matter is so crucial that I would like to offer Mr. Sturm some of my time, if we may do so without inviting mistrial."

There was another session at the bench. After a while a

clerk went out and re-appeared with a stack of huge books, at least seven of them, all of which were promptly opened; the courtroom whispered with the turning of pages. Slowly, Sam began to understand the point of Wlodzmierzc's carefully planted maneuver: it was for the jury a dramatic demonstration of utter confidence.

At last Sturm nodded and turned away. He seemed considerably shaken, but he advanced grimly on Sena.

"Miss Carlin, are you a geneticist?"

"No, sir."

"Have you ever had any training in genetics?"

"I have had one two-semester course, with Dr. Hammersmith of Dunhill."

"Did the late Dr. Hyatt personally tell you any part of the hypothesis you have just offered the court?"

"No, sir, as I told Mr. Wlodzmierzc."

"Have you checked the hypothesis, or any part of it, with the personal assistants of Dr. Hyatt whom you mentioned?"

"Briefly. Dr. Edwards agrees with it. Dr. Hammersmith was more cautious, and said only that it might easily be true."

"Did he state the reason for his caution?" Sturm asked drily. He was beginning to recover some of his composure.

"Yes, sir. He said that no-one really knows whether the 'normal' human being is tetraploid or not; that it was probable but that it would be extremely difficult to prove. If such a doubling occurred, he thought, it might have been one of the crucial steps in the evolution of *Homo sapiens*, and so took place an enormous long time in the past. He did add, however, that he had often discussed the point with Dr. Hyatt, and that Dr. Hyatt maintained that his experiments with us, the giants, were close to clinching it."

"We'll ask Drs. Edwards and Hammersmith to testify later. Will you state again whether or not the accused had any knowledge of this hypothesis?"

"I believe he did not," Sena repeated.

Sturm nodded to the jury. "Then it could not have affected his conduct on the day of the murder?"

"No, I don't see how it could have."

"Now, about those papers. Were papers relating *directly* to you among them?"

"Yes, but they were incomplete."

"And how about the accused, or Dr. St. George?"

"Those were missing in their entirety."

"Then you are unable to say *exactly* what your genetic status, Mr. Ettinger's, or Dr. St. George's might be; is that correct?"

"Quite correct."

Sturm straightened and said in a harsh voice, "Your honor, the prosecution feels that further pursuit of this aspect of the case would be fruitless. The prosecution thanks Mr. Wlodzmierzc for the courtesy of his time, and rests its case."

The judge looked at Sam's counsel. "Mr. Wlodzmierzc, has the defense any further witnesses to call?"

"Yes, your honor. We wish to bring the triploid dog Decibelle to the stand, demonstrating her intelligence by appropriate tests, and ask her certain questions of a nature which, as shown by the tests, she is capable of answering."

Sturm shot back to his feet, gesticulating wildly, but the judge was ahead of him.

"Mr. Wlodzmierzc," he said in a gravelly voice, "this is an American court of justice, not a side-show or a music-hall. The court has permitted you to introduce certain facts concerning this dog, but neither human patience nor the dignity of the law can countenance introducing this animal as a witness, capable of understanding an oath and testifying in a matter of life and death. If you have any further *admissible* witnesses to call, please do so. If not, this court is in recess for today."

The summations took all the next day, but the jury stayed out only six minutes.

XI

The effect of the verdict upon the public temper was astonishing, especially to Sam, whose knowledge of Roman history was about as extensive as that of any other layman —in short, zero.

Up to the first day of the trial, the question of whether or not Sam was guilty had not been much debated. It had been assumed generally that he was guilty, because it made a better story that way—a case of parricide, with pagan religious overtones patent to anyone familiar with Fraser or Graves. The actual guilty verdict, however, seemed to open up a wide gap in the populace; suddenly, the air was charged with dissension.

The letter columns of newspapers were filled with communications of all degrees of violence of language, each writer denouncing a previous one, and/or the stand of the paper itself. Fights over the subject in bars, sometimes involving all the customers, the barkeeps, the entertainers and the cops who came to restore order, became outright commonplace.

Clergymen unlucky enough to anounce "Atlantean" opinions—which most of them held—in predominantly "Titan" parishes lost their posts. Video commentators of opposing views raked each other recklessly over the coals. Congressmen made "Titan" and "Atlantean" speeches to their constituents while campaigning—sometimes gauging the prevailing opinions in their constituencies with great inaccuracy. Slanderous denunciations became too common to merit headlines any more, and "tetra" libel suits burst out with the frequency and violence of popcorn.

The whole complicated issue was further clouded by a heavy political coloration. For reasons not difficult to fathom, the general "Titan" viewpoint was adopted by most of the left-wing elements of the population, all the way from mildly pro-labor groups to militant socialists; the conservatives, on the other hand, espoused the "Atlantean" point of view, which was not only anti-Sam, but, unlike the team for which it was named, was also anti-giants too. Embarrassingly enough, the remnants of the American Communist party also adopted the "Atlantean" creed, claiming that the giants were laboratory zombies created to further capitalist schemes of world domination (a point of view apparently not shared by the Kremlin, insofar as anyone could guess what was thought there).

This coloration carried the bitter quarrel all the way into the home. Sons and daughters ordinarily took the "progressive" Titan line, while their parents registered stiff Atlantean disapproval. The subject was complex enough to nurture family splits as rancorous and as final as the theological hair-splitting which had been the bane of other ages.

Nor should any of this have been truly surprising. No wonder people debated the matter with passion. It was their immediate future as a race that they were arguing, as most of them seemed thoroughly aware.

Most of these developments Sam had to deduce, not without amazement, from the papers brought to him, while Wlodzmierzc was preparing his appeal. The first riot, however, he saw from his own window. A small labor union local had arranged a "Free Ettinger" demonstration just outside the prison, in response to the "Intern the Lummoxes" campaign which one of the yellower newspaper chains had been pushing. Similar demonstrations had already been held elsewhere in the city, all of them innocuous and, of course, ineffectual. (Besides, the chain was not really interested in the giants; it was using them, as it had once used the anti-vivisection issue for many years, in order to look militant without risk of alienating anyone of importance.)

But this march was outside the prison. The governor, a Titan himself, but ridden at home by an Atlantean faction, was in a bad state of the jitters. He committed the tactical error of calling out the militia against the demonstrators.

Most of the marchers were skilled workers in an engineering trade involving considerable training; they were peaceable, intelligent men in their forties, who would no more have stormed a prison than they would have taken to piracy on the high seas. The arrival of the state guard threw them into a state of high indignation. Furthermore, a mob of Atlantean factionists who had gathered to jeer at their Titan enemies got in the way, were shoved aside, and promptly began to stone the militiamen for interfering with their right of free assembly.

After that, Sam could not keep the two groups sorted out. There were shots, and tear gas, and men carried off in ambulances, and windows broken. The whole riot moved off from the prison, disappearing into the city proper, getting louder as it went; and inside the prison, a siren was howling—not because there was, or ever had been, the slightest chance of a jailbreak, but simply because the warden had been unable to think of anything else to do to assuage his excitement.

All of which, Sam knew, was only a prelude to holocaust. He went back to his bunk and waited for it to happen.

It began with a soft, hornet-like droning, not somnolent and soothing like the burr of bees, but with a harsh black edge on it, part hiss and part snarl.

Sam heard the angry midnight sawing for some time before it became distinct enough to be marked as a separate entity. He got up again and went back to the window.

He was aware that the sound had been going on for some time, but up to now he had not dissociated it from the rumble of the never-silent city. His heart and his breathing began to misbehave, and his mouth was very dry.

The future looked both short and violent from the black window. He had never, at any time, expected to be acquitted, but the court's refusal to allow Decibelle's appearance had killed the one real hope he and Wlodzmierzc had had—the hope of implicating Maurey sufficiently to impede him. Wlodzmierzc had agreed about the probability of a raid, and had indeed given Sam some explicit and shrewd pointers as to how to conduct himself if it occurred; but he had warned that only the dog could point definitely to Maurey as the real killer, and that Sam's own life hung from that probably inadmissable accusation.

A small, black clot, granular, like coal dust, was gliding

out of the horizon along the dully-lit undersides of the clouds. The humming grew steadily. So did the clot.

Sam wondered desperately why the local army base had not already been alerted. Surely they had searchlights and anti-aircraft weapons there. And what was the matter with the Air Force's radar net? Were they bored with the Un-identified Flying Object hysteria of the past decades suffi-ciently to dismiss anything that showed on their screens unless it was clearly a conventional aircraft or missile? A few jets in the air now would make all the difference—

But no lights went up, there was no sound of planes; the city, exhausted by the riot, dulled by a vaguely soothing video speech from the governor, snored. Belatedly, Sam realized that the humming sound was only just above the threshold of audibility—it sounded enormously loud to him only because it had meaning for him. If only he had, after all, told someone beside Wlodzmierzc—the warden, the court, anyone—the totality of what he knew to be coming; someone, someone would have believed him, or have been disturbed enough to sleep badly, to straighten now in his bed and ask himself, *What's that?*

Perversely, now that he had conceived the hope of its being noticed, the humming dwindled in Sam's ears and blended back into the somnolent droning of the city. For long seconds at a time he was convinced that he could not hear it at all. Then—since it had really not changed at all, except to come a little closer—it sprang back into being around his head like all the hornets of Hell's own ante-room.

The grains in the clot separated, became little black bacilli against the lurid culture-medium of the sky. The humming was now so heavy as to make Sam's eardrums flutter uncomfortably; he realized suddenly that it was too loud for the apparent distance of the swarm. Lights were coming on in the city, too, and somewhere deep in the prison there was a hoarse shout of alarm—not the shout of an official, but that of a trapped man being approached by a doom he cannot even understand.

The humming swelled again, growing so suddenly almost to a roar that Sam ducked involuntarily. When he looked out again, a swarm of clearly identifiable human figures, silhouetted inkily against the sky, was pouring through the

air over the prison—was pouring *away* from him, toward
that other cloud which had come from the horizon.

A thin spear of monochromatic yellow light stabbed
from the clenched fist of one of the near-hurtling shadows.
There was a flat crack, not nearly as sharp as the sound of
a gun, but somehow reminiscent of thunder, all the same.
Immediately, there was a fusillade of them.

The more distant, oncoming group responded at once.
No sound could be heard from it, but the flying cloud was
stippled with yellow stars. At the same instant, Sam's eyes
were filled with stone-dust, and a fearful blow across his
skull, just above the left temple, slammed him reeling away
from the window.

In the darkness, his head ringing, his gritty eyelids burning, the bitter truth drove in upon him. There were "Atlanteans" and "Titans" among the giants, too. Maurey obviously had whipped up a predominantly Titan group to
staging his raid on the prison—but the Atlanteans, in surprising strength, had gotten there first.

A pitched battle, a civil war in the air, was already
under way—and not just between giants and diploids, but
between giant and giant.

He stayed away from the window, his eyes watering. He
had no idea of the power of the version of the one-way
push which the flying squads were using as a weapon—the
gaudy spears of light, he deduced, were stigmata of the
adaptation of the principle to stadium use—but as its dis-
coverer he knew already that it would be effective over any
distance, limited only by the horizon. The accidental, random hit on the window, from some shot fired by the still-
distant Titans, had given him a more than adequate reminder of that.

Raging, he patiently blinked away the dust and watched
the development of the New Pasadena from the far side of
the cell, through an embrasure of the apparent size of a
postage stamp. The noise of the city was up a little, a
drone-bass for the stuttering implosions of the giants' side-
arms. A sudden wavering rib of light, appearing and disappearing in the field of the postage stamp, told Sam that
the airfield, at long last, had come awake, and was groping
for the cause of the disturbances in the sky.

At once, a whole series of heavy impacts struck the
near wall of the prison. The shouting of the invisible pris-

oner rose to a wail; then it was drowned out by the prison siren—apparently the siren was the warden's only answer to all problems. Another series of blows followed, battering the stone with a sound like the merciless hammering of age-split hollow logs.

The Titans were taking no chances. Now that the threat of discovery from below had materialized, they were not wasting more than a few shots upon their indistinct Atlantean brothers. They were bombarding the prison, an object which they had some chance of hitting. It was even possible that they had little to fear from the Atlantean attack except at very close quarters—if both sides were using tournament weapons, they probably both had effective armor against those weapons; Kelland would have been careful about a thing like that. The stone walls of the prison, on the other hand, would soften in a hurry under a reactionless bombardment.

The sirens howled on, completely obliterating all sounds from outside. But the shocks against the outer wall could still be felt.

Then the corridor lights went out.

Sam spun and stared. A maddening square illusion, about the size of a postage stamp, floated in front of him wherever he looked. It took a long time to fade, but finally he was sure. The lights were really out—all out—

Even the warning light which showed that the bars of the door were electrified.

Somebody had been sufficiently frightened by the bombardment to pull the master switch.

The electrically operated locks which kept all the cells closed would still be in operation, of course, powered by an independent "hurricane" generator. But the charging on the bars had been just a jury rig from the main lines. Sam grappled for the bars, and after two swipes, one sweating palm closed around cold steel. No lethal shock convulsed his muscles.

Bracing himself, he began to pull.

The door was tough. It seemed immovable. Then, it gave, just a little. His hand slipped; he wiped it on his prison dungarees and took a fresh grip, this time with both hands.

He was not going to be "rescued" by Maurey St. George if he could help it.

He got to work on another bar, dragging it painfully in the same direction as the first. There was no chance that he could get two of them far enough apart to allow him to squeeze between them; they were too close-set, and bending one meant bending all, since they were all bound together in a two-dimensional sheaf by four flat cross-pieces. But if he could bulge the whole cagework enough to drag the lock down and out of its socket—

The siren died abruptly. But no lights came on, and no searing shock raced through the bars. The invisible prisoner was weeping convulsively. Outside, the crepitations of the giants' weapons came through loudly; and now, too, there was an occasional, heavy *blam*.

Anti-aircraft shells. Momentarily, Sam was faint with horror. It seemed impossible that any armor Kelland had designed would be proof against that.

Sam pulled. The hinges ground against the stone. One corner of the door scraped protestingly against the concrete floor. Sam bent double, siezed that corner, and forced it out and toward the center of the cell—

With a coarse screaming, the bolts sheared. The thousands of foot-pounds of drag testing their small cross-sectional strength had told. The door came inward—against its normal direction of movement—about seven inches. Sam crammed himself between it and the wall, shoving with all his strength—

And was out in the corridor.

BOOK THREE

XII

Kelland pulled an edge of the blind away from the window, with the delicate movements of a man who half expects the material to tear in his hand, and peered with one eye around it out at the dim, eventless woods. Then he sighed, let it fall to, and turned on one shaded lamp.

"We're on the spot, Sam," he said heavily. "I did my best to keep those tee-total damn fools from staging that raid, but I couldn't get a soul to listen to me. I'm just supposed to design weapons and play dumb about what's done with them. Anyhow, you were lucky to get away, and I'm glad to see you. Is there any hope for salvaging anything?"

"I don't know," Sam said carefully, easing his burning feet out in front of him. He had run most of the way to Kelland's isolated, ramshackle house in the exurbs, after he had managed to fight clear of the panic around the prison and get out of the clogged center of the city; no heart but a giant's could have stood up under that slogging, brutal marathon, and even Sam's was pounding against his ribs like a kettledrum stick. "There may be. I was hoping that you wouldn't be part of either party on the raid, but I wasn't sure. I'll confess that I came close to bursting into tears when you opened the door to me."

"That's all right," Kelland said, his own feet suddenly seeming two sizes larger. He shifted in his chair. "Forget it. How about a drink? You look so winded, you scare me."

"Um, I don't know. I guess I'd better. If you have a little brandy—"

"Yes, sure, some Courvoisier? Or a Fundador?"

"Either, just go it lightly. This evening isn't over by any means."

Kelland fetched and Sam took a cautious sip. It was marvellously heartening. Kelland sat down again and said, "Where's Maurey—do you know?"

"No, don't you?" Sam said, astonished.

"No, Sam. He was supposed to lead the Titans to the prison, but he never turned up. They waited for him about half an hour, and then someone came in shouting about an Atlantean counter-raid. They all took off in a complete rabblement. A fanatic named Briggs—I think you remember him, the tetra who did Methfessel's first propaganda work?—well, he took Maurey's place. I didn't like anything about the proposition, so I went home instead, but I've been following it all through the transcaster."

Sam groaned. "And here we sit, waiting to be arrested, while the giants help the diploids to destroy us all! Kelland, you built all this apparatus; I don't know to what uses you modified my principle. Isn't there any step you can suggest?"

"Well," Kelland said cautiously, "I can at least get up to date on how the fighting is going." He got up and took down a golden helmet from a high bookshelf. "You needn't worry too much, you know, Sam. That force of yours has polarity—don't look so flabbergasted, did you ever encounter a field that *didn't* show polarity?—and I took the trouble to make direct connections between the armor and the projectors. They can't do much more than stun each other, even up close—"

"All right, all right, but they'll be massacred by the diploids when they come down!" Sam shouted. "Bullets don't carry charges to be repelled by like charges!"

Kelland looked alarmed and settled the helmet on his huge head.

"Briggs? Briggs! Ah; good. This is Kelland. Did you lose anybody to the anti-aircraft shelling? . . . My God. Well, maybe that's not as bad as it might have been. Good thing you had sense enough to get out of the air when you did. Why don't you pull out entirely? . . . You *have?* But great God, Briggs, there's no sense in that—Sam's escaped. Get out of that concrete tomb before somebody puts the lighs back on. . . . Never mind the Atlanteans. They can hear me as well as you can. They know Sam's gone. Think about the future of the giants for once! Get out before the diploids trap you in there. They may decide to blow the whole place up, guards, prisoners and all, just to trap you in there. . . . Dammit, Briggs, you're a fool, and a giant fool is the worst kind of fool that there is. Get everybody out of there while you've still got power. The diploids will trace the plant to here sooner or later, and if you're in the air *then* it'll be a long fall!"

Sam sat bolt upright. Kelland looked at him, raising his eyebrows resignedly, lifted the helmet and held it delicately between his fingertips.

"They're in the prison," he said, "fighting with the Atlanteans and the diploids, but he isn't sure about our own losses. I can't seem to get any sense into his head. He doesn't believe that you're out. You'd almost think he wanted to liberate you himself, he's so eager to locate your cell."

Sam let that pass. *"Can you cut off their power?"* he whispered.

"Why, sure," Kelland said, turning the helmet round and round reflectively. "I didn't think it safe to power each suit individually. Neither did Methfessel. We wanted a way to ground both teams if tempers got lost and the tournament showed signs of turning serious."

"Where's the generator?"

"Right here, under the house. It was easy to install, it's not much bigger than a desk. They pick up the broadcast from the helmet transcaster—the little Christmas tree you see here."

"Kelland," Sam said grimly, "give me that helmet!"

Puzzledly, Kelland handed it over, and adjusted the cheek-mike to Sam's face. Sam said into it: "Briggs, you've got five minutes to get out of there."

"Mind your own business," a harsh voice snarled inside Sam's skull. "You chose to stay home. We'll conduct our business without you—and remember you afterwards. Right now, keep your nose clean, or. . . ."

Briggs' voice trailed off. When it came again, it was shockingly different.

"Ettinger, is that you?"

"That's right," Sam said calmly. "Your boss has run out on you, Briggs. He's snitched Sena for himself, and left you all to massacre each other. What you all fail to do to each other, he thinks the diploids will finish."

"You're lying!"

"Oh? Did you read the records of the trial? Don't you know why Maurey wants Sena? And why he wants the rest of us dead? But it's too late for you to begin thinking;

you're rusty; I'd better do it for you. Get over here, to—the power source. Fast. All of you. That includes Atlanteans. Five minutes, remember; at the end of that time, I'm going to have Kelland switch the whole fool lot of you right out of the sky."

"You dirty butcher."

"Not I," Sam said, almost cheerfully. "I'm giving you a break you don't deserve. But be sure you're—over here—before the five minutes are up. After that, your pop-guns won't pop any more, and your flying belts won't fly. *Git!*"

He took the helmet off. Kelland's eyes were bugging.

"Are you nuts?" Kelland demanded. "They'll flay you alive for the threat alone. Half of them already think you're a traitor. And you didn't give me a chance to tell you—but every tetra wearing one of my suits heard every word you said. Are you trying to commit suicide along with the rest of us?"

"No. I wouldn't have bothered to say anything into your helmet if I'd thought I was talking only to Briggs. Anyhow, I'm not going to be here when they arrive, Kelland. I've got other business. I want Maurey."

"I heard that part of it, too. I don't think I believe it, though."

"I didn't believe it either, at first," Sam said soberly. "But it's true. He's the one who killed Dr. Fred, not I. He found out, accidentally, that our polyploidy was very mixed in nature, and that the way its manifestations will occur in the generations to come is also going to be mixed. It was Sena's records that drove the point home to him, and I think it hurt his sanity. He wanted the giants always to be *giants*, always obviously superior, always able to lord it over other humans in the most visible possible way. He planned to avenge Pasadena by running it in reverse—by wiping out the diploids with the weapon I gave him.

"But after the trial, he knew that that could never happen. He knew that the future lay in the assimilation, and the gradual reappearance, of polyploid characteristics among 'normal' people. That was what Dr. Fred had planned for; he didn't tell us because he knew it would hurt us, after all we've suffered because of our size, but that was the way it was going to go. And will go."

"And Maurey?"

"I think he decided right away to short-circuit the

scheme, by ditching the obvious giants—by trapping all of them into destroying each other, with the happy collaboration of the diploids—while he, Dr. Maurice St. George, superman, sets himself up to become the father of all the future."

"Ugh," Kelland said. "The hell of it is, it might still work."

"No, I don't think so. It's already falling apart. There's very little left to him for his pains now, except for Sena. As long as he can hide her, he can protect himself, he can be pretty sure, from the present, and be patriarch of all the generations to come. But he can't hide her, Kelland—because she's mine."

He stopped to ponder for a moment. "Kelland, tell the diploid police this; we'll need them. But not until our own people get here and you can make them understand what's at stake. Give me one of those helmets and I'll report back as I go, so you can all follow me when the time comes. We'll have to smoke Maurey out ourselves, but we'll need the diploids to make it good. And we'll need to show them that we're acting in good faith."

"You'd better take the whole armor," Kelland said, even more gently than before. "Maurey will be armed with it, too, and there'd be no point in your being killed by your own discovery, when protection's available."

"Okay."

"But Sam," Kelland said. "You haven't answered my question yet. Excuse me, I guess I haven't asked it yet. But—"

"What is it? Go ahead, Kelland."

"How do you plan to find her—and him?"

"She's been staying in Dr. Fred's old vacation shack. Right?"

"Right. And, God help me," Kelland suddenly cried, "he got me to bring Decibelle down here tonight, so Sena was all alone when he kidnapped her!"

"Kidnapped? Not exactly. I think he just moved in. Dr. Fred had moved all his papers up there after Maurey opened his safe. Even if Sena weren't there, that's where Maurey would have had to go. He would hide himself among those papers; it's the only way he thinks. I should know."

"I blame myself," said Kelland despondently. "I should

have known that about the shot Decibelle had to have was just a ruse."

"Well, to answer your question, Decibelle will take me—wherever they are."

Kelland looked stunned. "The dog has changed, Sam. She almost went for the vet when he set the needle tonight. I tell you, *I* was scared."

"Of course she's changed. She's almost full grown now. she's an old friend of mine. I doubt if she's changed to me; and if I tell her we're going to Sena—"

Kelland's answering, delighted smile irradiated the room.

"Yes, Sam. Of course she is still your friend. Go ahead, I'll do as you say. I think it'll work. Your friend is—hell, man, just go to the door and call!"

Sam strode to the door and threw it open upon the frosty night. Behind him, Kelland added: "And—good hunting, Sam!"

Sam called:

"Decibelle! Decibelle! Come to Sam! Come to Sam! Decibelle—here, here, to me! Decibelle, here to me!"

There was a glad and thunderous barking. Sam went out into the night to meet her.

XIII

The forest was tar-black, and itchy with the small night-movements of an old woods in a populated and resorted area, the movements of creatures too small to tempt hunters and too adaptable to care where they lived, the movements of tattered leaves and scrub wood, of mice, squirrels, sparrows dreaming, barn owls hunting, roaches, moths, midges, all the noise of regrowth after too-heavy timbering.

Decibelle tugged. Sam knew approximately where Dr. Fred's shack was, and, though he had never been there, probably could have found it in daylight by himself. But the urgent need now was to get to Maurey—before the inevitable marshalling of diploid justice against the insurgent giants set Maurey free of the trap he had woven around himself. And not only for the protection of the giants; but for the protection of Sena, who was their future.

Hence, Decibelle, at four o'clock in the morning.

He stumbled over something which might have been a root. It was hard to tell, because the pressorfield disturbed his footing. Trying to recover, he slammed face first into a treetrunk.

The golden casque clanged. Dazedly, Sam righted himself, holding the dog back with difficulty. On his back, the heavy flying apparatus hung uselessly, like a vulture bending to peck at his liver. The pressorfield was useless for collisions of this sort, cushioning the blow not at all, since all its pressure was out and away from Sam, none of it back to him. It could shove branches out of his way, and protect him from mosquitoes, but it could not push over a tree; instead, it flowed around the tree and pushed him into it from behind. It was wholly recoilless, it would push only one way, and that was that.

So much for invincible weapons, Sam thought. *They lack discrimination.*

131

The pull along the rawhide which connected him with Decibelle continued, and Sam let it draw him. That impact on the casque had been rather heavy. Better see if the radio was still alive. He pulled the cheek-mike over.

"Kelland?"

"Present," the earphones said at once, amid the forest murmurs.

"Good. Kind of thick going here. Kelland, do you have any foreign language?"

"Uhm. Will French do?"

"No," Sam said. "All I know about French is that it forms plurals with soundless X's sometimes. Besides, Maurey speaks it, and I don't care to have him know what I'm up to. You don't by any chance speak German?"

"Doch gewiss," Kelland said, shifting immediately into that language. *"Aber ein bischen bejudelt.* My family name was Keller, until I changed it to keep the tetraploid stigma off my relatives; Jews have enough to bear, without that. But Maurey—?"

"I doubt it," Sam said. "German is a chemist's language, not a physicist's—Beilstein and all that. I owe my own knowledge of it chiefly to a boyhood enthusiasm for Wagnerian opera. The enthusiam didn't stick, but the language did. Good enough. Now, what's going on back there?"

"Nothing much yet. People are still coming in, and I'm saving my breath to explain it all at once to everybody," Kelland said. "Any further instructions?"

Sam stumbled and swore. Then he said, "Well, give them the whole story, and try to keep them in hand until I find Dr. Fred's place. I'll call you all over here after I see how the land lies. Leave behind a cadre to defend your power source, or we'll all be sunk without a trace. And, oh, yes, as soon as you can, send off a couple of our biggest boys to kidnap somebody in authority—an Army officer, preferably, or a state cop. Equip the prisoner with a helmet, so he can hear what we're saying and follow whatever develops, but don't of course give him any flying equipment or pistol. Bring him along when I yell for help. Got all that?"

"Um," said Kelland, in the voice of a man who is taking written notes. *"Erzäahl' Geschichte . . . stehl' Sicher-*

heitsdiener (that covers all categories, doesn't it, Sam?) . . . *gib' Helm . . . stell' Hindtreffen.* That about it?"

"*Jawohl,*" Sam said, and then, "*Ouch!* I'm going to shut up for a while. Decibelle seems to be drawing me through a jungle-gym made of barbed wire."

"All right. Hello, here comes Hammy Saunders. I'll sign off too, since I'll have to speak English for a while to explain things to the assembled company. But I'll keep the earphones on."

Sam pushed the mike away again and said, "Hey-Decibelle?"

Rrrrrgrrph.

"All right. Go ahead. I'm with you."

Decibelle obviously was not tracing out any path the brittle Dr. Fred could have taken to his lodge by custom. These mountains were ancient and much worn down, so much so that visitors from the Far West usually affected not to be able to see them at all, but even so Dr. Fred would have needed an open path, without any steep grades, winding around the bases of the hills.

The dog, on the other hand, at the moment was dragging Sam sidewise out of a creek-bed full of brambles, and on up the side of a crumbly rock shelf. Obviously, she was taking him along the way she herself went to the lodge, when unencumbered by human company. It was both a compliment to Sam and one more evidence of Decibelle's ability to assess an urgent situation for what it was.

Sliding and scrambling up the hill with all his aching tendons creaking, Sam was able to notice that there was a little of dawn on the sky. Not enough of it had leaked through the trees, down below, to have given him fair warning.

The dog was pointing. She had never been trained to point, but evidently she had once seen a trained dog assume the odd position and had figured out what it was for. Her mimicry would have won her no prizes at any show, for her hackles were up and her ears laid back, but Sam was hardly inclined to be a purist about it.

"Good girl," he said softly. "It's on the other side of the crest, eh?"

Decibelle's tail wagged once and straightened into the "point" position again.

"Good. Lie down, Decibelle. Stay here. I'll be back."

Sam scanned the dim hill carefully and then lay down himself, working himself up the slope on his belly. At the top, he cocked one eye cautiously over the summit.

The other side of the hill sloped more steeply, and the shack clung to it, looking out over a placid and lovely valley with a stream at the bottom. This slope was grassy; and at a radius of twenty yards from the shack, the grass bent away in a perfect circle. A pressor-field.

Sam considered the problem. It was about what he had expected to find. He knew, as well as anyone knew, the characteristics of the reactionless effect. Since the field worked only in one direction, it could be used as a shield, but *not* as a detector. Force exerted against it had no effect upon its generator; the field did not push back, eiher physically or electrically. That meant that the only road to perfect security for Maurey was an unremitting, twenty-four hour optical watch, either in person or by a video watchdog. If Sam kept out of sight, Maurey would have no way of knowing whether or not anyone was in the vicinity.

Maurey, of course, had heard the German conversations, but had no way of knowing what they meant. He might have guessed that he was in danger of being smoked out; on the other hand, the fact that he had chosen Dr. Fred's lodge as a hideout—and the existence of the pressor-field showed that he had—was a clear indication that he did not expect anyone to suspect the place. The screen was routine; it would baffle diploids, but Maurey could not have expected it to baffle the giants for long.

He simply had not expected Sam to figure out where he was hiding. In that he had overestimated himself and—for the last time—seriously underestimated his former assistant.

Sam withdrew a few feet and called Kelland.

"We're all here, Sam," Kelland's voice said. "And we've got our Authority. We had a little trouble with Briggs, but he lacks Maurey's deviousness. He tried to sell the rest of us on Maurey's program by talking about the necessity of Dr. Fred's death. It made convincing the rest of us very easy; we have Briggs salted away."

"You can come on over," Sam said. "The place is on the side of a hill overlooking the valley on the far side of the old deer preserve. If you come in on it from the north and fly low, he won't be able to see you until we're ready."

"Sam!"

The voice was Maurey's. It sounded cool and amused.

"I've been listening to you. Whatever in the world made you think I couldn't speak German?"

"All right, let's hear you speak some," Sam said.

"Don't be ridiculous. You've made a big enough fool of yourself already; you don't even recognize your friends. They've freed you, and you can't think of anything better to do with your freedom than hatch infantile plots with poor Kelland, who can be convinced of anything."

"Where are you?" Sam said.

"I'll tell you that when I can depend upon your common sense, not before. I'm not going to endanger the whole project for one man who doesn't know when he's well off."

"Where's Sena?"

"She's right here with the rest of us. If you want to have any part in the world of the giants, Sam, you'd better have some sober second thoughts. Our patience is about worn out; in a little while we'll have to go ahead without you— and I don't suppose the little obsolete folk will deal kindly with you."

With an almost inaudible hum, a shadow drifted in front of Sam, and Hammy Saunders landed lightly beside him. Sam said:

"You could be right. It's happened before." He pushed the mike away again. Maurey's grandiose fictions continued to purr in his ears.

"Hammy, he's got the place surrounded by a field. We'll have to undercut the rock below. Send three or four men down into the valley, under cover, and get to work on the hill with pistols, just below the effective limit of the screen. Don't start mining till I say 'when,' though."

"Right."

Hammy melted away. Sam sat on the hillside next to the dog and watched the dawn colors brighten, pulling sweet clover and sucking the nectar from the tight white flower-clusters, cold with dew. Maurey seemed to have signed off, at least for the moment.

Kelland and two other giants came humming in, dragging with them a frightened diploid in civilian clothing, ridiculous in outsize golden helm. Sam took one look and whistled.

The man was the governor of the state.

"Sicherheitsdiener covers a lot of ground, all right," Sam said, amused in spite of himself. "Sir, I'm sorry for this apparently senseless abduction, but believe me, we mean you no harm. We mean no diploid person any harm. We're here to smoke out the one giant among us who's created the trouble, beginning with the murder of Dr. Hyatt. We've been forced to bring you along as a witness to our intentions, and how we implement them."

The governor was grey with terror, but he had an inherent dignity which stood him in good stead. "I'm forced in my turn to accept that, for the moment," he said stiffly. "I'll watch and listen, since I'm powerless to do otherwise. But you may as well know that I don't believe you."

"There's no necessity for that. If you watch and listen with an open mind our case will prove itself. You've already heard my conversation with Dr. St. George. He's over the hill, in a shack that used to be Dr. Hyatt's summer lodge. He's holding one of us with him, the 'Titans' Daughter' about whom you've heard so much: Miss Carlin. He doesn't know yet that we're anywhere in his vicinity. When we turn him out, you may hear more than enough to give you the full story; at least, that's our hope."

"There are militia scouring the whole countryside for you!"

"We know that; that's why we're here. Had the militia arrived before us, had we told the militia where Dr. St. George was and why we wanted him, there would have been a number of deaths—including Miss Carlin's. He's well equipped to stand off any normal siege, except one conducted by bombing or heavy artillery, which would destroy him and Miss Carlin without proving a damn thing. We mean to convict him out of his own mouth, with no loss of life. Doesn't that strike you as a preferable way of going about it?"

The governor passed a hand heavily across his forehead. He was swaying a little.

"Perhaps so," he said. "If there's any truth in it at all. I'm in no position to be judicious. I've been kidnapped by agents of a convicted murderer—you, Mr. Ettinger. My view of whatever it is that you plan will have to be colored by that situation. Go ahead. I'll pay close attention; that's all I can promise."

"That's quite enough," Sam said gravely. "Your recog-

nition of your bias is also the assurance I need that you'll
not be swayed by it. Kelland, see if you can find a vantage-
point for the governor that'll be out of the way of any
possible fireworks, but will still allow him to see everything that happens. He's the most important person in this
show, far and away, and ought to be guarded accordingly."

"Right," Kelland said. "Governor, we'll have to hale
you through the air again—for the last time, I hope."

"So," said the governor, "do I."

They went away, Kelland leading, followed by the two
giants with the small ineffectual figure of the governor between them, skimming the tree-tops in a wide arc toward
the opposite side of the valley. The sun was coming up on
the left, reaching gradually into the valley itself; a great
many birds were making a musical bustle. There was actually a small curl of woodsmoke coming up over the brow
of the hill from the shack, blatant, self-confident, innocuous.

After a while Hammy came back.

"The boys are working on the hill under the lodge," he
said. "It seems to be mostly soft marl. No alarm from
Maurey, nor any sign of suspicion at all, yet. If everything
goes right, the shack ought to begin to totter in about ten
minutes."

"Good," Sam said. "You jumped the gun on me a little,
but it shouldn't matter now."

He got to his feet and began to climb, unhurriedly, his
face calm, his fists clenched. He went over the brow of the
hill and stood looking down on the lodge. Decibelle followed, and sat down beside him.

"Maurey," he said into the cheek mike, "you've been
found. We'll give you ten minutes to come out of there."

Maurey began to laugh.

"Out of where?" he said. "Sam, what a child you are!
Did you think you could get away with that 'I know where
you're hiding line on *me?* If you want to know where we
are, I'll tell you; but not before I'm sure you won't sell us
all out to the diploids."

"There are no human diploids," Sam said patiently, "and
you've been found. Come to the window, Maurey, and
look up the hill."

There was quite a long silence.

"I see," Maurey's voice said at last. "Well, I suppose no

refuge is perfect. And I suppose you've got a great howling mob of diploids on your trail. You'd best send them back, Sam, before they get hurt. Don't imagine that a shack on a hillside is all that remains of tetraploid power."

"I don't. I don't imagine that you've any great army of giants in there, either, Maurey."

Maurey chuckled again.

"This place is bigger than it looks," he said. "But I won't argue with you. I retain some shreds of respect for you, Sam; and I recommend most strongly that you pull out before the final battle breaks. It's all over for the diploids; nothing that you can do can change that. Why get hurt?"

"There are no diploids," Sam repeated. "Where is Sena?"

"Sena?" Maurey said. "Why, here, with the rest of us."

"I'd like to talk to her."

"She's busy."

Sam moved one hand. The hillside, the ledges of the valley, the hillocks, the grasses uttered giants; they stood everywhere, motionless, like the dragon's-teeth soldiers of Cadmus.

"Here are the giants, Maurey," Sam said. "You can see them, if you'll look. There are only two or three missing, at the most—not counting those that were caught or killed in your raid on my prison. One of the missing is Sena. Where is she?"

"She's here." Maurey's voice was as confident as before; there was nothing in it to indicate that a bookcase-full of his own lies had just fallen forward upon him, though the shock must have been considerable.

"Let her out."

"She doesn't want to come out. She's got more sense than all the rest of you put together. I don't know how the hell you sold your brothers on this stupidity, Sam—I suppose Briggs got killed, I can think of no other explanation offhand. Killed trying to rescue *you*, Sam. Anyhow, there's no essential change in the situation. If all the rest of you have sold out to the diploids, Sena and I will work out the proper destiny of the giants without you. Go home and rot, all of you!"

"There are no diploids," Sam said. "Let us talk to Sena."

Maurey was silent. After a while it seemed that he was

not going to speak again; then, startlingly, his voice came back, loudly, urgently:

"The rest of you," he said. "Listen to me. You're committing suicide. You had power over the diploids in your hands, and you've given it over to the man who murdered your creator. I gave you a cause; I gave you the means to be free of the pygmies, truly and finally free. Are you going to give all that up now?"

"Briggs said *you* killed Dr. Fred," a voice that Sam did not recognize said. There was no other way of telling which of the gigantic gilded statues had spoken.

"What does that matter?" Maurey demanded. "Be realistic! I didn't kill Dr. Fred; obviously Sam did. You all know how hard I worked to defend Sam, but all the same Dr. Fred's death was quite necessary. It provided us with the chance we needed to arouse the diploids against us. Dr. Fred preached peace with the pygmies. We all know that no peace was possible. What was needed, what's needed now, is war. You have the instruments for that war in your hands, and on your backs. I gave them to you, and intelligently used they're invincible. And you have the occasion. You could sweep the planet clean."

"You divided us," another anonymous voice said. "You made us fight each other."

"Harmlessly," Maurey scoffed. "You can't hurt each other with the force-pistols. I saw to that. Naturally I also saw to it that you quarrelled with each other—there was no other way to disguise the raising of a private army of giants. But your weapons are deadly only against diploids."

A whisper, eerie and disembodied, came from among the statues.

"How about the anti-aircraft guns, Maurey?"

"Well, how about them? Your losses were tiny, Sam himself admits that."

There was a low rumble from the giants.

"Too bad, Maurey," Sam said, implacably. "The truth is out, you see. It came out at the trial. *There are no diploids.* All human beings are tetraploid. We—the giants—are polyploid, but we're all polyploid in different degrees. As giants we won't survive; but we can survive through Sena and others like her, because Sena's children will look normal. They'll be able to blend back into society, and they'll allow *their* children to conceal their heritage, even forget it, perhaps. Eventually the polyploid characteristics will begin to reappear, piecemeal, until the whole race is heavily polyploid, and then giants will be commonplace and not the subject of pogroms.

"But as for you, Maurey: *You are a Pasadentist.* A subtle one, but a Pasadentist all the same. You found out about Sena, and you killed Dr. Fred to keep that a secret. You pitted us against each other, in the hope that the normals would destroy us all while we were snarling at each other. Pinning the killing of Dr. Fred on me gave the normals reason to hate us, and staging the raid on the prison gave them reason to wipe us all out—

"While you hid here, with Sena, planning to become the sole father of the polyploid humanity of tomorrow—sole forefather of the tough, long-lived race that will be needed to reach the stars.

"It was a good gamble, Maurey. But since it was insane, it failed."

Maurey said, "Ridiculous."

"Then let us speak to Sena. If she's free and on your side, she has a helmet and has been hearing everything that was said. Let her speak."

"Certainly," Maurey said, calmly. "As I remarked before, she's busy. I'll see if she wants to talk to you. Hang on."

Silence. The sunlight was now almost down to the bottom of the valley, where Hammy's sappers were worrying the foundations of Dr. Fred's lodge. The clouds were pink with innocence.

The silence stretched out, and for the first time of which he was aware, Sam began to worry. There was something unsettling about the calmness with which Maurey clung to his story and his course, as though it were indeed possible that he and he alone was the only loyal giant and the rest of them traitors and fools. And since even he would hardly go so far as to let Sena speak, he must be using these moments in some other way—

"Here she is."

"Here she is."

"Sam?" Sena's voice said quietly.

"Yes. . . . yes, Sena."

"I'm all right. There's no reason for you to worry about me at all. He's got a gun on me—"

Sena stood with her arms easily bent, her fingertips just barely touching, like a concert singer waiting effortlessly for the applause to die down, or like a Williamsite at prayer. If she had never truly joined the congregation, she was at one with them now. She had granted Maurey every possible liberty of belief and conscience, and had been unspeakably afraid, until she realized that he was no longer worthy. Now she merely watched him with an impregnable calm.

He had tried to lash her with words into his own excitement. "What do the others matter? It's you and me, Sena, and I'll get children on you that will rule the world after us—after us, the deluge; hah!—remember Noah? *He* slept with his own two daughters to remake the world and I wouldn't mind the chore, myself."

It was loathesome to hear his magnificent speaking voice echoed by his own tittering. Sena laced her fingers a little tighter together, and stared him down, meeting the brown glitter of his eyes with her own frosty blue.

It was almost more than she could endure to see him lose even that control. His stare went wall-eyed like that of a stallion being led from a burning stable. "You don't," he said, "you don't think I'm strong enough, to make you follow my orders. I am much stronger than you think, I can make anything follow my orders. I can—Look!"

He had laid his hand on the top of the pot-bellied stove, and she could smell his scorching flesh. Her nostrils widened a little, and she said, "I pity you."

He had snatched his hand away, and made as if to slap her with the blistered palm, when Sam's voice again distracted his attention. Maurey held the helmet to his chest as if it were something he had removed while riding in an elevator, as if he might put it on again when the trip was over, or sling it on a convenient hatrack.

She listened to his broadcast counterfeit of sweet reason, the tone he no longer bothered to take with her, and then he was offering the helmet to her, forcing her to sit at right angles to him, using Dr. Fred's plain deal table as a kind of stool on which she must lean back with both her palms flat on the wood while he slipped the helmet over her head.

He was very careful to stay out of the range of her legs, which he had made a contemptuous point of not binding in any way, and he was careful to keep the gun on her throughout the hissed instructions, but he was rough with the helmet and it caught on the golden knot of hair at the nape of her neck. "He's got a gun on me—" She tensed to swing her legs up when he charged.

"—but he won't dare shoot—"

On the last hurried word her voice faded abruptly, and Sam's earphones shivered. Maurey must have thrown the helmet across the room. His answering gasp was half fright and half sheer admiration. She had said so much in so few words—

"Speak up, Maurey!" he shouted. "Any last lies?"

"Keep your distance, all of you," Maurey said. His voice was tight, frigid. "You're a pack of fools. Just remember that you're outside, and I'm inside with Sena. Sam's quite right! Sena's the key; if the giants are to survive at all, it has to be through her. And if any one of you makes a move toward the lodge, she'll die. Understand?

"She was right, too! I didn't kill her for squawking; I only—removed—her helmet. I don't kill for little things. I kill for reasons only. Like Dr. Fred. So go away. Your future is in my hands—and there's nothing you can do about it!"

Suddenly, the lodge seemed to cant, and then sagged sharply to the right. A mass of rubble went thundering and foaming down the hillside into the valley. Maurey's incredulous scream made Sam's ears ring.

The flat-lying circle of grass stood up, and began to ripple tentatively in the morning breeze.

The failure of the foundations had cut Maurey's power-line.

"Decibelle! Get him, Decibelle! In the shack! Quick Decibelle *get Maurey!"*

The immense animal charged toward the lodge, impossibly low to the ground. A force-pulse shot out from the sliding structure, but it was high.

Decibelle launched herself and went through the small pantry window in an explosion of glass. Maurey screamed

again. Sam found himself running; he would have flown if
he could, but he didn't know how to use the apparatus.

Another bolt from inside the lodge blew planking out-
ward in a fountain of dust and splinters. Still another
never got outside at all, but the chimney tottered and collapsed, dumping hot bricks on the roof.

*"Take her off! Take her off! I'll kill you all, I'll kill you
all—*

Maurey had his dog at last.

Before Sam was much more than half-way to the lodge,
the hillside beneath it gave way completely, and Maurey,
logs, bricks, fire, Sena, future, past, dog, plaster, dirt, concrete, planks, pipes, wires, life pursuit and happiness slid
in one big untidy chaos toward the pineneedle floor of the
valley, just ahead of the sun's fingertips.

It took a little while to separate Sena's just-living body
from the wreckage.

It took longer to separate Decibelle from the ruins of
Maurey's throat.

But after a while the giants were gone, and the shaken
governor too; and the sunlight touched the valley, all the
way down to the stream where the wreckage lay, and began to climb back up the slopes.

If you like Heinlein, will you love Van Vogt?

A READER'S GUIDE TO SCIENCE FICTION

by Baird Searles, Martin Last, Beth Meacham, and Michael Franklin

Here is a comprehensive and fascinating source book for every reader of science fiction — from the novice to the discerning devotee. Its invaluable guidance includes:

*A comprehensive listing of over 200 past and present authors, with a profile of the author's style, his works, and other suggested writers the reader might enjoy

*An index to Hugo and Nebula Award winners, in the categories of novel, novelette, and short story

*An outstanding basic reading list highlighting the history and various kinds of science fiction

*A concise and entertaining look at the roots of Science Fiction and the literature into which it has evolved today.

"A clear, well-organized introduction."
Washington Post Book World

"A valuable reference work."
Starship

AVON Paperback

46128/$2.95

GSciFI 6-81 (2-9)